QUARANTINE

HARPER  PERENNIAL

NEW YORK • LONDON • TORONTO • SYDNEY • NEW DELHI • AUCKLAND

QUARANTINE

STORIES

RAHUL MEHTA

HARPER ● PERENNIAL

HarperCollins books may be purchased for educational, business, or sales promotional use. For information, please write: Special Markets Department, HarperCollins Publishers, 10 East 53rd Street, New York, NY 10022.

FIRST EDITION

Designed by Justin Dodd

Library of Congress Cataloging-in-Publication Data is available upon request.

ISBN 978-0-06-202045-1

11 12 13 14 15   OV/RRD   10 9 8 7 6 5 4 3 2

for my father, mother, and brother
for my grandparents,
in memoriam
and
for Robert

ACKNOWLEDGMENTS

I am full of gratitude for the many, *many* people who have provided encouragement and support over the years and who have had faith in me even when I didn't. A complete list would rival in length the short story collection itself. But I would like especially to thank the following:

My agent, Nat Jacks, for finding me, for being patient with me, and for believing in me.

My editor, Rakesh Satyal, for his generous and incisive readings of my work and for his unflagging enthusiasm (no one could ask for a better editor); his assistant, Rob Crawford; Katie Salisbury; Joseph Papa; and all the other wonderful folks at Harper-Collins.

The tremendous team that launched my book in India: Chiki Sarkar, Rachel Tanzer, and Sohini Bhattacharya.

All the editors who have published stories from the collection: Diane Williams at *NOON*; David Lynn at *The Kenyon Review*; the editors at *Fourteen Hill*; Colleen Donfield, Andrew Snee, and Sy Safransky at *The Sun*; Michael Koch at *Epoch*; Rajni George at *The Caravan*; and Kathy Pories and Madison Smartt Bell, for selecting my work for the anthology *New Stories from the South*.

The students, faculty, and staff in the Syracuse University Creative Writing Program for sharing their tremendous talents with me, particularly my classmates Stephanie Carpenter, Phil LaMarche, Monique Schmidt, Nina Shope, Christian TeBordo, and Erin Brooks Worley; my teachers Bob O'Connor, Arthur Flowers, Brian Evenson, and Mary Karr; and my amazing, *amazing* thesis adviser and hero, George Saunders.

All the additional readers whose feedback helped shape this manuscript, especially Anne Coon, Gail Hosking, and Susan Morehouse.

John Laprade and Kate Hawes, for somehow managing to make me look, in my author photos, a little less like the total dork that I am.

Erin Brooks Worley, whom I've already thanked, but must thank again (and again and again and again . . .) for invaluable critiques and for the birds.

My family, both immediate and extended, in the U.S. and in India, especially my parents, Kunj and Nalini Mehta, and my brother, Nimish Mehta, for support beyond anything anyone could ever expect; my uncle and aunt, Shirish and Nita Parikh, for generously providing time and space for me to complete this collection; and my cousin, Sodhan Parikh, for the New Year's Day phone call that did more for me than he could know.

And, of course, my partner, Robert Bingham: exacting editor, astute critic, and love of my life.

CONTENTS

ONE

Quarantine

Y ou will only see him the way he is, not the way he was."
Jeremy and I have rented a car and are driving to my
parents' house. He has never been to West Virginia. All
week he has been looking forward to seeing the house where I
grew up, my yearbooks, the wood paneling in the living room
where I chipped my tooth, the place by the river where I drank
with friends. He is annoyed that I am talking about Bapuji again.

"Don't you think I know by now how you feel about your
grandfather?" he asks.

"Yes, but I am warning you. When you see him, you will feel
sorry for him. You will forget all the stories I've told you."

"I won't forget."

"You won't believe me."

It is late by the time we reach the house. My parents hug me at the door. They tell Jeremy how much they enjoyed meeting him in New York last year. They are awkward. They half hug him, half shake his hand. They are still not used to their son dating men.

"Make yourself at home," my mom says to Jeremy.

"Bapuji is in the living room," my dad says to me.

We remove our shoes and go inside. Bapuji is sitting in a swivel chair. The lamp next to the chair is off. In the dim light it is difficult to see him, but when he stands up and comes closer, I see how loose his face is, the deep dark eye sockets and sharp cheekbones, the thin lips oval and open, as if it is too much effort to close them or smile.

I bend down to touch his feet. The seams on his slippers are fraying, and his bare ankles are crinkled like brown paper bags. He lays his palm on my head and says, "Jay shree Krishna." Then I stand and he hugs me, my body limp.

"This is my friend Jeremy," I say. Jeremy nods and Bapuji nods back.

Last week when I called my mom to discuss plans for our trip, she said it was better not to tell Bapuji that Jeremy is my boyfriend. "There is no way he could understand," she said.

My mother warms up some food and, even though they are leftovers, Jeremy and I are happy to have home-cooked Indian food, to be eating something other than spaghetti and microwave burritos. After dinner, my mom tells us we can make our beds in the basement. She and I spoke about this on the phone, too. She said we shouldn't sleep in the guest room because there is only a double bed there, and it will be obvious we are sleeping together. Better we set up camp in the basement where there is a double bed and a single bed and a couch. She said "camp" like we are children and it is summer vacation. She hands us pillows and several sheets of all different sizes and says she is going to sleep.

I make the double bed for Jeremy and the single bed for myself. Jeremy suggests we both sleep in the double bed and that we can mess up the single bed to make it look like one of us slept there. "I don't think it's a good idea," I say. "What if we sleep late, and someone comes down and sees us?"

As we are falling asleep, Jeremy asks, "Why did you touch your grandfather's feet?"

"It's a sign of respect."

"I know, but you don't respect him."

"I respect my father."

"You didn't touch *his* feet."

"Don't be funny," I say. "He is Americanized, he doesn't expect such formalities. But if I didn't do pranaam, it would hurt my grandfather's feelings, and that would hurt my father's feelings." A few seconds later I add, "It's tradition. It doesn't really mean anything."

"Yeah, tradition," Jeremy says, sighing, sleepy-voiced. A few minutes later, I hear him snoring from across the room.

Whenever I see my grandfather, I have to touch his feet twice, once when I first arrive and again as I am leaving. Each time I hold my breath and pretend I am bending over for some other reason, like to pick up something or to stretch my hamstrings. He always gives me money when I leave, just after I touch his feet. I never know what to do with it. I don't want to accept it, but I can't refuse. Once I burned the money over my kitchen sink. Another time I bought drinks for my friends. Once I actually needed it to pay rent. But it didn't feel right. It was dirty, like a bribe.

Now, as I try to sleep, I toss and readjust, trying to get comfortable. I am not used to sleeping alone. I don't know what to do with my body without Jeremy's arms around me.

The basement where we are sleeping is where my grandfather lived when he first came to America. I was ten then, and Asha was eight. Bapuji came a few months after his wife, Motiba, died. At first he tried to live on his own in India, but he found it too difficult. He couldn't take care of himself, didn't even know how to make tea. He shouted so much that whenever he hired new servants they would quit within a couple of days. In the end, my father took it upon himself to bring Bapuji to America. As the eldest of five brothers and sisters, he thought it was his responsibility to take care of Bapuji, which, I quickly learned, really meant it was my mother's responsibility.

My mom says Bapuji wanted to live in the basement because the spare bedroom upstairs was too small and he needed more room. After I left for college he moved upstairs into my old bedroom, which was bigger than the small spare.

When Asha and I were young, we'd hardly ever go all the way into the basement. We'd only go partway down the stairs and hang on the railing like monkeys and spy. The basement smelled of Indian spices and Ben-Gay. Bapuji made my mom hand wash all his clothes, because he said the washing machine was too hard on Indian cloth and stitching. He didn't like the smell of American detergents. He made her scrub his clothes in a plastic bucket with sandalwood soap and hang them to dry on clotheslines he strung across the room. He tacked posters of Krishna and Srinaji to the walls, and he played religious bhajans on a cheap black cassette recorder that distorted the sound, making it tinny and hollow, as though it were coming from far away.

Rahul Mehta

Asha and I called the basement Little India and my grandfather the Little Indian.

Those early years in a new country were difficult for him. He barely spoke English, and there were no other Indian families in our community. He couldn't drive, and our housing development wasn't within walking distance of anything. He wasn't used to the cold. Even in the house, he would have to bundle up with layers of sweaters and blankets and sit in front of a space heater. Now and then my parents would try to take him to the mall or the park, but there was nothing he wanted to buy and he claimed that Americans looked at him funny in his dhoti and Nehru hat.

But if it was hard for him, he made it equally hard for everyone else, especially my mom. She took a couple of months' leave from her job in order to help Bapuji settle in. He made demands, and as far as he was concerned she couldn't do anything right. He wanted her to make special meals according to a menu he would dictate to her each morning. He insisted my parents add a bathtub to the basement bathroom, even though they couldn't afford it and there was already a standing shower. He would call my father's brothers and sisters and tell them his daughter-in-law was abusing him, that she was lazy and disrespectful and a bad housekeeper. He would say his son shouldn't have married her. When my mother was cooking in the kitchen, he would sit at the table and say, "This isn't how Motiba made it."

Years later, my grandfather even claimed that my mother was trying to kill him. Bapuji was a hypochondriac, always complaining about his health, aches in his joints, a bad back, difficulty breathing. He had started complaining about chest pains. My mom was sure it was heartburn. She said she had seen him sneaking cookies and potato chips from the kitchen cupboard late at night. She said he should stop eating junk food and then see how he feels in a couple of weeks. But Bapuji called everyone, my aunts and uncles, even relatives in India, saying his daughter-in-law was refusing to let him see a doctor because she wanted him dead.

When my mother told Asha and me Bapuji claimed that she was trying to kill him through neglect, I said, "If only it were so easy."

"You shouldn't joke like that," my mom said. But then I looked at Asha and Asha looked at me and we both started laughing, and my mother laughed, too.

My mother and father often argued about Bapuji, never in front of us, but we could hear them shouting in their bedroom. Sometimes they'd go for a drive, or sit in the car in the drive-way. Once after a tense dinner during which my mother served Bapuji rice and dhal and Bapuji looked at the plate, dumped all the food in the garbage, and went to the basement, my mother took my father onto the back porch. Asha and I peeked through the window blinds. It was winter, and my parents hadn't put on coats. We couldn't hear what they were saying, but they were pointing and pacing and when they spoke their words material-ized as clouds.

On the Saturday evening after Jeremy and I arrive, Asha vis-its us with her husband, Eric. They live a couple of hours away and are both in med school. Jeremy and I spend the morn-ing in the kitchen helping my mom roll and fry poori.

After dinner we play Pictionary as couples: Dad and Mom on one team, Asha and Eric on another, and Jeremy and me on the third. Bapuji sits in a corner while we play.

Asha and Eric are winning, mostly because Asha is so good at drawing. When we were kids, she drew the most beautiful pictures, mostly horses. She loved horses. They were so good my mother framed a couple and hung them in the living room. My drawings were terrible. I threw them away without showing them to anyone.

It is Asha and Eric's turn, and the word is "snatch." Asha guesses it quickly, but when I look at Eric's drawing I am horrified. He has drawn something vulgar. I hold up the picture and show it to my parents and say, "This from a future doctor." My mother giggles and blushes as though she is twelve. I tell Eric and Asha that they should be disqualified from the round because the category is "action" and he drew a noun. Eric says he can draw whatever he wants, as long as the person guesses the right word.

"Uh-uh," I say. "Look it up. It's in the rules. Plus, your drawing was rude, so you should lose two turns." Everyone is laughing and arguing. My grandfather comes over to see what's going on.

"Do you want to play?" Jeremy asks him. I look at Jeremy like he shouldn't have done that, and he shrugs.

Bapuji shakes his head no.

"Then you should go sit down," my mother says. "Otherwise, it's too crowded around the table."

Bapuji goes back to his chair. Two rounds later, we are all racing to see which team guesses "diminish" first. It's in the "difficult" category. My mom is frustrated because it *is* difficult, and it is her turn to draw for her team and my father is guessing all wrong. "Look!" she says, pointing emphatically at her paper. "Just look what I've drawn. Look what's here. Can't you see?" Bapuji comes over again, and he is leaning over my mother's shoulder looking at her drawings. He starts to guess "little" and "smaller" and my mother says, "Please go sit down." She continues drawing and he continues guessing "tiny" and "shrink," hovering over her, leaning closer and closer until his chest is touching her back. My mother slams her pencil down on the table. "Bapuji," she shouts. "Please, just quit it!"

We all stop. Bapuji looks around at us. Then he walks over to the swivel chair and sits down. After a couple of minutes, he collects his shawl and goes upstairs without saying good-night.

No one wants to play Pictionary anymore. Asha suggests we watch one of the movies my father rented. It is a big-budget comedy, one that I would never rent, about a man and a woman who don't like each other at first, but end up falling in love. The movie is formulaic, the dialogue horrible, but the actress has such a stellar smile and the actor is so goofy and good-looking, we are all charmed. We laugh loudly at the bad jokes. We guess the ending, but the predictability is comforting, and we are all smiling as we tidy the living room and prepare for bed.

The next morning Asha and Eric leave. My father challenges Jeremy to a tennis match. He is eager to show off the fancy country club with the indoor courts that he joined last year. He's always wanted to join, ever since he came to this town.

My mom and I go to a café by the river for bagels and coffee.

"I'm sorry I made a scene in front of Jeremy," she says.

"It's no big deal," I say. "It seems like things are getting better, though. For you, anyway. I've noticed Bapuji mostly spends time in his room now. Not like when Asha and I were kids and he followed you around the house, barking orders."

My mother takes a sip from her coffee. "I don't like who I am when he's around. I don't like how I behave. I know I am mean sometimes."

"You're not mean."

"Do you know what it is like to have someone living in your own house who hates you?"

"He doesn't hate you," I say.

"It would be easier if your dad would take my side. When we're alone he says yes he understands, yes Bapuji is difficult, yes he disrespects me, but he doesn't say it to Bapuji. He doesn't stand up to him."

"How can he?" I say. "Bapuji is his father."

"I am his wife."

I finish my bagel and coffee and my mother pays at the cash register. When we get in the car in the parking lot, she says, "Forget it. I'm sorry for bringing it up. I want to have fun with you and Jeremy before you leave." She puts her hand on my knee for a minute, then starts the car.

I was sixteen the year my mother's father died. She hadn't seen him in years. She got a call from Bombay that he was ill, and left the very next day. By the time she arrived, he was dead.

When she returned, she was different, quiet. She didn't go back to her job right away. She stopped cooking. She spent most of the time in her room with the drapes closed.

My father tried to keep house. I helped, too. We took turns cooking dinner: burned rice, overcooked vegetables with too much chili pepper and salt. After ten days, Bapuji said to my father, "How long is this going to last?"

"I don't know," my father said. He was rummaging in the fridge.

"It is her duty to take care of us. You must tell her."

"Her father died."

"My Motiba died. You didn't see me behaving like this. She is selfish. She has always been selfish. Why must we suffer because of her?"

My father picked up the phone and ordered pizza.

I went upstairs to my parents' bedroom. The door was slightly ajar, and I wondered if my mother had heard them talking. I knocked twice and she didn't answer. I opened the door fully. It took several seconds for my eyes to adjust to the darkness. My mother was lying in bed on one side, the covers pulled over her head.

"Are you OK, Mom?" I asked, still standing in the doorway. She didn't answer. "I'm worried. Please, Mom. Do you want to go out? I can take you for a drive. Maybe some fresh air. We can get buckwheat pancakes at IHOP."

My mother was silent. I walked toward the bed, and as I approached I could hear her crying beneath the covers. I stopped, not sure what to do. I wanted to put my hand on her shoulder, sit on the edge of the bed stroking her the way she would stroke me when I was a kid and I was sick or upset. But I didn't. Instead, I turned around and left, pausing for a moment in the doorway. "I love you, Mom. Please get better."

A couple of days later, my mother returned to work. She started cooking again, but she still didn't talk much, and she didn't smile. I saw her standing at the stove one evening, stirring the dhal. My grandfather was sitting at the kitchen table, watching her.

I want to take Jeremy on a road trip. There is a town seventy miles up the Ohio River, famous for three things: ancient Indian burial mounds, after which the town is named; a state penitentiary; and a large Hare Krishna commune.

When I was young, my family visited the commune often. It is beautiful, set atop a hill with views of the river valley. There is a temple and a Palace of Gold. My family went a couple of times a year to worship. In those days, there were no Hindu temples nearby, and my father figured the Hare Krishnas were the next best thing. But my mom was wary. She thought they were weird.

"This isn't our religion," my mother said.

"Krishna is our god," my father said.

"These people aren't our people," my mother said.

When we had visitors from India, my father always took them to the Palace of Gold, which the Hare Krishnas called "the Taj Mahal of the West."

One summer, he tried to send Asha and me to summer camp at the commune. He showed us a brochure. He said he wanted us to learn something of our culture, to understand where we came from. But looking at the children in the brochure, their white faces blank as they sat in the temple while a white man in a saffron robe read from a book, I couldn't understand what my dad meant. Asha, on the other hand, was lured by the pictures of kids riding horses. In the end, my mom refused to let us go. Even Asha, who had seemed so excited, was relieved. She was nervous the Hare Krishnas would shave her head.

Now, as Jeremy and I plan our trip, my father warns us the commune isn't what it used to be. He says there was a murder a couple of years ago, and the head of the commune was arrested for tax fraud and embezzlement. Still, I insist on showing Jeremy.

It is my father's idea to invite Bapuji.

"He'll get in the way," I say. "We'll have to stop every five seconds so he can pee."

"C'mon," my dad says. "He hasn't been to temple in years. Besides, he can use an outing."

I tell my dad I'll think about it. Later, Jeremy says to me, "If we stay late it will give your mother a break from your grandfather. Think of it as a favor to her."

The three of us drive up the valley on the two-lane road. We drive through one-light towns with old church steeples and country general stores, and picturesque hills broken only by the spitting smokestacks of the chemical plants that have proliferated along the river.

When we reach the town, it is even more depressed than I remember. The penitentiary was shut down a couple of years earlier when the state ruled that the prisoners' cells were too small, that keeping inmates in such cramped quarters was cruel and unusual punishment. Many people lost their jobs. The town is still suffering.

To get to the commune, we have to take a narrow road that snakes up a large hill. It is separated from the rest of the town. Both the Hare Krishnas and the town's residents prefer it that way.

The Hare Krishnas own the whole hill, including the road. It is in such bad condition, I have to drive extra slowly. The sign for the temple is so faded I almost miss it. Once there were cows on the green hills and white men with shaved heads wearing necklaces made of tulsi beads, and women in saris with hiking boots and heavy coats in the winter. Now the hills are empty. Many of the houses are boarded up. The cows are gone.

Our tour guide at the Palace of Gold speaks with a Russian accent and explains how, in Moscow, under the Communists, he had to practice his religion in hiding, at secret prayer meetings. He is lucky to be in America, he says.

The palace isn't heated, and Bapuji shivers beneath his layers—

two flannel shirts that don't match, two crewneck sweaters, a heavy jacket that once belonged to my dad. He pulls the coat collar closer to his neck.

Outside, much of the gold leaf has flaked off the structure, and inside there are cracks in the ceiling. The marble and wood need polishing. One stained-glass window is broken. The tour guide tells us we should come back in summer when the rose garden is in bloom. "It's really beautiful," he says.

After the tour we eat a late lunch with the devotees. There are only a dozen of them, and we all sit silently in rows on the floor eating off stainless steel thalis. The food is modeled after Indian food, but it is nothing like my mother's. It is bland and tasteless—beige and brown and gray.

When we go to the temple, the alcoves with the statues of gods are all covered with velvet curtains. A devotee tells us they won't open them until the aarti at five o'clock. He says we should stay. Jeremy and I decide to take a walk around the commune, and Bapuji says he'll wait in the temple. He is talking to the devotees when we leave him.

Jeremy and I find a pond flanked by fifty-foot-high statues of Radha and Krishna dancing. Their hands are joined in the sky, forming an archway. Small cottages, modern-looking with large windows, surround the pond. I tell Jeremy that one year my father wanted to rent one so we could visit on weekends, but my mom refused. I tell him there used to be peacocks. We walk around searching for them. We find deer and swans and rabbits, but no peacocks. Not even a feather.

When we return to the temple, the aarti has already begun. The curtains have been lifted, revealing a gold statue of Krishna in the center and Hanuman and Ganesh on either side. They are layered with garlands and surrounded by candles. My grandfather is standing in the front of the room before the statue of Krishna. To our surprise, he is leading the aarti, chanting "Hare Krishna, Hare Ram." He is holding a large silver platter with coconuts and flowers and a flame and burning incense, and he moves the offering in clockwise circles. He seems too weak to carry such a heavy platter. I wonder how he is managing. Everyone is watching him, following him, echoing his chanting. Jeremy and I sit in the back silently.

Afterward, several devotees talk to my grandfather. They want to know about India. Are the temples beautiful? Has he been to Varanasi or to Mathura, birthplace of Krishna? He is smiling and gesturing and he has more energy than I have ever seen. It is only with great difficulty that we are able to pull him away.

When we return to the car, it is almost dark. Bapuji is quiet again, moving slowly. I ask if he wants to sit in the front seat. He shakes his head no.

After twenty minutes in the car my grandfather says, "I want to go back."

"We are going back," I say.

"No," he says. "To the Hare Krishnas."

"Did you forget something?"

"I want to stay there," he says.

"You can't," I say.

He taps Jeremy on the shoulder so that Jeremy turns around, and then he whispers, "I am not happy."

Jeremy looks at me.

"Don't talk nonsense," I say.

The road winds around a corner and I can see the moon reflected on the river up ahead. After a couple of minutes, Bapuji says again, "I want to go back."

I grip the steering wheel tightly, and my shoulders tense. "Be quiet, Bapuji."

"Your friend understands me," he says, tapping Jeremy on the shoulder again.

"He's not my friend," I say. "We are a couple, like you and Motiba were."

Bapuji is silent for a few minutes. Then he says, "Your mother is a bad person." "Do you want to talk about bad people?" I say. My hands are shaking. "You are a bad person. You are the worst person I know. You have caused nothing but pain in my family."

"Be careful," Jeremy says. "Watch the road."

"Your life is nothing anymore. Look at you. Pathetic. Let my mother be happy."

I look in the rearview mirror and see my grandfather's face in shadows. It catches the light from a streetlamp, and through his glasses I can see his eyes and cheeks are wet and he is trembling.

Jeremy screams and grabs the wheel. I hear a horn and look forward and see flashes of light.

When we finally come to a stop, our car is in the grass beside the road facing in the wrong direction. A car honks loud and long as it passes us, and the sound disappears in the distance.

I flip on the overhead light and look over at the passenger seat. Jeremy is OK. He is staring at me, trying to catch his breath. I look in the backseat. I can see my grandfather's seat belt is fastened, but his head is down, his chin on his chest. "Bapuji?" He doesn't respond. "Bapuji?"

I get out of the car and open the back door. I put my hand on his shoulder, shaking him gently. Even with all the layers of clothes, his shoulder is thin and narrow. My grandfather looks up. His glasses have fallen on the floor and the lenses are cracked.

"Are you OK?" I ask. He nods.

I walk around the car a couple of times to see if there is any damage. We try the engine, and it starts. Jeremy drives the rest of the way home.

When we reach the house, Bapuji goes straight to his room.

"Is something wrong?" my dad asks.

"He's probably tired," I say.

My mother asks us if we are hungry, and we say we already ate. I tell them I am tired and we have to leave early the next morning so we should go to sleep. Even though it is early and it is our last day, my parents don't argue. My mother says she is tired, too.

A few years ago, while I was away at college, Bapuji contracted tuberculosis. At first, we couldn't figure out how he got it. We had never heard of anyone getting TB in America. Then my father remembered that Bapuji's younger brother had died from it when they were both children. The doctors said Bapuji must have been exposed to the bacteria then, and that it had been dormant in his system all these years, waiting for his body to weaken, waiting to attack.

For the first few days of his illness, Bapuji was quarantined in the house. He wasn't allowed to leave his room except to take a bath and use the toilet. The doctors said he could be dangerous to others. They advised my parents to limit their contact with him, and not to let anyone else enter the house. Later, when his health got worse, he was admitted to the hospital and isolated in a room with special ventilation. Whenever anyone visited, they had to rub antibacterial liquid on their hands and forearms and wear masks and gloves before entering the room, and they could only stay for a short time.

My mother visited the most. She brought him homemade

food during lunchtime and sat with him every evening. My father came less frequently. My mother said it was too difficult for him.

One weekend, I flew home to visit my grandfather. Just before going to the hospital, I gulped coffee and ate nachos. When I put the mask on, I couldn't believe how vile my breath was. I couldn't escape it. I thought, *This is what's inside of me.*

Bapuji seemed disoriented and didn't recognize me at first. He was tired. The mask must have made me look strange.

In the car, on the way to the hospital, my mother had told me that when Bapuji's brother was dying of tuberculosis, and he was miserable and in pain, Bapuji would let him rest his head on his chest, and sing to him until he fell asleep. This is how Bapuji got exposed to TB. I couldn't quite picture the scene. Such tenderness didn't fit with the grandfather I knew.

Bapuji said he needed to use the toilet. My mother helped him to the bathroom. When he got up, I noticed a brown stain on his bedsheet. His gown was open in the back, and I could see a bit of dried excrement on his backside and his skin peeling like birch bark. I remembered my parents telling me the TB medication made his skin dry.

When Bapuji was finished, he called for my mother, and she went into the bathroom and helped him clean up. I buzzed for the nurse to change the bed.

Watching my mother, I realized this could be her future: he could fall seriously ill, and she could spend many years taking care of him. My mother also knew this. I could tell by the matter-of-fact way she went about her tasks—cleaning him, rinsing his drinking cup, flipping his pillows—the blank look on her face while she did them, as though she were the one fading away.

.   .   .

Jeremy and I wake early the morning we are leaving my parents' house. We eat cereal while my mom makes sandwiches for our car ride. She has cooked some extra Indian food for us to take with us, and she puts the curries and subjis and rotis in a small cooler and sets them in the foyer next to our luggage. "Everything is cooked. All you have to do is heat it up when you're hungry."

We are all standing in the foyer.

"I'm glad you guys came," she says.

"Me too," my dad says. "Bapuji!" he shouts up the stairs. "The boys are leaving."

It is silent upstairs. My father shouts again, "Bapuji!" Still nothing.

"He is tired," I say. "Let him stay in his room. I'll go up."

His bedroom door is shut. I knock, but he doesn't answer. I open it. The room is dark. Bapuji is in bed. His broken eyeglasses are on the bedside table, on top of the Bhagavad Gita. He has the covers pulled over his head.

"Bapuji," I say, quietly, "I am leaving." He doesn't answer. He is either asleep or ignoring me.

I remember so many years ago, my mother in bed after her father died, the covers pulled over her head, me approaching, hearing her cry, not sure how to comfort her.

I remember also my grandfather's story about comforting his brother as he was dying.

Now, I don't approach my grandfather. I don't know whether he is crying under the covers. I stand in the doorway another minute, watching him, and then I leave.

When I go downstairs, my father asks if I did pranaam, and I say yes.

Jeremy drives most of the way home. We don't talk much. I fiddle with the radio, which usually annoys him, but today he doesn't say anything.

Back in New York, our apartment smells terrible, like we forgot to take the garbage out, or something died between the walls. Even though it is cold out, we open a couple of windows.

I walk into the living room to open another window, and I see the answering machine is blinking the number eight. I figure some of the messages are from my friends or from Jeremy's friends, but I'm sure some are from my family. Probably my mom or dad. They'll want to know we arrived safely. Maybe one is from Asha. Maybe there is one from my grandfather. I don't play the messages.

I go into the kitchen, take my mom's food from the cooler, and put it in the freezer. Jeremy is in the bedroom unpacking, and I can hear him opening and closing dresser drawers.

"Are you hungry?" I ask.

"Starving," he says.

Jeremy wants some of my mom's Indian food, so I take out a couple of Tupperware containers and pop them in the microwave.

As for me, I can't stomach it. I reach for a box of spaghetti and set a pot of water on the stove to boil.

TWO

Floating

His clothes make me think he is one of us. Form-fitting T-shirt, Diesel jeans, leather loafers with contrast stitching and square toes. It is an outfit I would wear.

Later, I will notice he wears the same clothes every day. Later, I will notice the holes.

We meet him our first day in town. We are at the café waiting for pancakes and porridge, a reprieve from the heavy curries we have been eating for days. The food and the décor—sleek European modern—make us feel we are somewhere else, except for the café's open front, which faces the street, and exposes us to its sights and sounds: a woman crouched with a bundle of sticks, sweeping; a feral dog begging for scraps, skittish from being beaten, but hungry enough to beg nonetheless.

He is sitting with a cup of tea at a nearby table. He asks me the time. He says his name is Rajesh. I say, "I'm Sid. This is Darnell."

Rajesh says he likes my notebook, the one covered in raw silk. I say, "I bought it at Target." He says, "Such a beautiful color."

Darnell invites him to join us, and Rajesh slides over. Our pancakes and porridge arrive. Nothing comes for Rajesh.

"I ate earlier," he says.

The way he looks at our food, I know this isn't true.

As we start eating, Darnell reminds me it is time for our Larium, and I fish two pills from my daypack, one for Darnell, one for myself. I also swallow a Pepto-Bismol prophylactically.

Rajesh asks us, "Where are you from?"

"America," Darnell says.

Rajesh says to me, "But you look Indian."

"My parents are."

"You are not?"

I shrug. "And you? Where are you from?"

Rajesh gestures up the street. "I have lived here all my life."

I say, "When I first saw you, I wouldn't have guessed. I would have thought maybe you were from London."

"Thank you," he says, "Maybe someday . . ."

He asks how long we are visiting, and Darnell says maybe a few days, maybe a week or two. "You must advise us. What should we see? Where should we eat?"

"What do you like?"

"Pizza," I say.

Darnell says, "You come to India and all you want is pizza and pasta and vegetable lo mein."

Rajesh says there is a restaurant nearby where I can get pizza. He explains it is owned by the same man who owns the café, a

German tourist who came many years ago and never left. The restaurant is called Savage Garden. I raise my eyebrow when Rajesh says this—the use of the word "savage" by the German seems wrong—but Rajesh doesn't seem bothered, his tone is flat. He says Savage Garden the way I say Olive Garden. I say, "Aren't you offended?" He says, "He is a nice man."

I think I remember seeing him, the German, sitting in the café just before we met Rajesh. Darnell had pointed him out: a fat man in a silk kurta accompanied by a young, handsome Indian man.

I open my notebook to copy the address of the restaurant. As I am flipping to find a blank page, Rajesh notices a sketch.

"Who drew that?"

"An artist we met in one of the palaces in Jaipur," I say. "We took a tour. He had a stall."

Rajesh says, "Were his paintings good?"

"Typical," I say. "Mostly miniatures, in the Mughal style, painted on parchment and silk, the kind you see everywhere. His were better than most. He drew this elephant in my notebook because he wanted us to buy a painting. He came from a long line of artists; he was proud. He said the men in his family had been artists for four generations, that they had painted portraits for four generations of maharajas, and all these paintings were hanging together in the maharaja's private residence."

When I am finished telling Rajesh about the artist, he asks to see my notebook. He finds an empty page and pulls a ballpoint pen from his back pocket. Quickly, he sketches a small elephant, very different from the one the artist in Jaipur drew. Compared to the fine brushstrokes of the Jaipur artist's elephant, Rajesh's elephant is a cartoon. "I am an artist, too," he says.

Darnell says, "Very nice."

"Soon I will start classes at J.J. School of Art in Mumbai."

Rajesh says the school's name in a grand voice, as though we should be impressed. I am. I know the school. It is famous.

"My paintings are on the Internet," he says. "A French couple bought some. They own an art gallery. There is a website. When you have time, we can go to an Internet café together, and I will show you. Do you read French?"

Darnell and I shake our heads.

"Maybe I will go to France," Rajesh says. "I will bring the French couple more paintings."

After a few minutes he says, "Let's do this. We are friends. I will show you around and help you with everything you need while you are here. Any sights you want to see, any food you want to eat, any people you want to meet—I will help you. Then, one day you can come visit me at my house. We will have tea, and you can look at my paintings. If you like, you can buy."

I don't know what to say. I don't want to buy anything. I had made a promise to myself.

A month before we came to India, some friends of ours, having recently returned to New York from a trip to Kenya, invited us to their apartment for dinner. They cooked steamed cornmeal and collard greens with cubed beef and said, "This is a traditional Kenyan meal." They showed us photographs from their trip. On the living-room floor, they spread out all the items they had brought back: batik wall hangings, soapstone statues of stylized human figures with long necks and ear-lobes, wood carvings of giraffes and gazelles. With each item, the couple told an accompanying anecdote: one about being in the bazaar and having to bargain fiercely with a one-toothed woman, another about wanting to buy a set of wooden serving bowls but being directed to a shop that sold lingerie instead.

Rahul Mehta

They called the items "artifacts," and invited us to pick one. We chose a soapstone pencil cup.

That night, on the subway home, holding the soapstone pencil cup, I told Darnell, "I don't want to return from India with a suitcase full of trinkets and funny stories to tell my friends. I don't want to be that kind of tourist."

"What kind of tourist do you want to be?"

"I don't know. But maybe if I don't buy anything, I can find out."

Darnell tells Rajesh now, "We would love for you to show us around."

We don't want anyone to know where we are staying. We are embarrassed. But everyone asks—the shopkeepers, the waiters in restaurants, the young men loitering outside shop fronts—and the town is too small for us to lie.

I can see their faces change when we tell them. They don't understand. They have seen the hotel's marble façade, the silver-and-glass mosaics of peacocks flanking the entrance, the turbaned doormen who stand all day in the heat. They have heard about the rooftop swimming pool with the three-hundred-sixty-degree view of the city. How can I explain to them that, to us, it is not expensive? I want to say, *Back in America, I eat ramen noodles and peanut butter sandwiches every day. We are not rich.*

We wouldn't be able to afford the hotel were it not for the drought. It is the monsoon season, and the rains are heavy everywhere but here. The town has had bad luck for several years in a row, leaving its main tourist attraction—the lake—bone-dry for the first time in thirty years. Tourism is down, room rates slashed. Even then, we had to bargain.

The other reason we are able to afford the room is because my parents are paying: a detail that bothers Darnell, uncomfortable about taking money from his boyfriend's parents.

I tell him not to worry. I tell him that forty years ago, they, too, visited this city, on their honeymoon, and someone else paid: my mother's father.

Because of the drought, and the drop in tourism, the shops are empty. Everyone is idle. The drivers outside our hotel recline in the backseats of their auto rickshaws. They shout to us as we walk by, calling out popular tourist destinations: "Jagdish Temple. Sunset Point. Sixty rupees only." They are disheartened when they see we have rented bicycles. They laugh at the floppy sunhat I wear reflexively from years of my mother telling me to stay out of the sun, warning, "If you get too dark, no one will want to marry you."

Outside our hotel we meet another boy, about the same age as Rajesh, and an artist, too. He introduces himself as Carlone. When I ask about the name he says it is after a character from *The Godfather*. "My father took inspiration from him." Carlone puffs out his chest. "So do I."

I have never seen or read *The Godfather*, and I do not know who Carlone is or what he does. I do not know if he is a hero or a villain, whether he is sympathetic or not. But I do not trust this Carlone.

He has a shop just across from our hotel, which he keeps with four other young men from his village. He calls them his brothers. He is the leader, because he speaks the best English. They all live in the shop and sleep on the floor at night. They have no customers, so they spend all day sitting out front in plastic chairs.

Every day as we bicycle back and forth, Carlone shouts, "When will you come see my shop? When will you come have tea?"

One day he stops us by stepping in front of our bicycles. "Please come in."

"We are in a rush," I say.

Darnell is less brusque. "Your shop looks new."

"It is. We have been here less than a year. Before that, we were farmers in the village. Then there was no money, so we left and came here. Please come in. Look at the paintings."

"We are not interested in paintings," I say. "We are not going to buy. I don't want to give you the wrong impression."

"At least you can look. At least you can drink tea with me."

"We are late meeting someone," I say.

Carlone knows Rajesh has been showing us around town. Everyone knows. As we are bicycling away, he says, "Why do you go with that boy?"

Darnell says, "Why not?"

Carlone says, "It isn't right."

Rajesh wants to show us the town's three famous palaces: City Palace, where the maharaja spent his winters; Lake Palace, where he summered; Monsoon Palace, where he weathered the rains.

The most spectacular, by far, is Lake Palace. It is long and marble, and is designed to look like it is floating in the middle of the lake. But with the lake dry, the effect is ruined. The palace looks bloated and beached. The boats that normally ferry guests back and forth from the palace to shore have been replaced by camels and elephants and Tata SUVs. In the dry lake bed, we see children playing cricket, families picnicking, cows grazing.

Rajesh tells us the palace was converted into a hotel shortly after Independence, when the British left India and the maharaja had to find alternate forms of income.

I already know about Lake Palace, because it is where my parents stayed on their honeymoon.

I also know about it because it is prominently featured in a James Bond movie, *Octopussy*, which I saw as a child with my parents. My parents rarely took me to movies, not wanting to spend the money. But they were proud to see India in a major film, even if the portrayal was somewhat unflattering, the Indians clownish.

Octopussy is shown every night in town, at one hotel or another, advertised on wooden signs outside the establishments. One of the hotels uses the original movie poster, with Bond standing, holding a gun, three women hidden behind him, their arms extended, so that he looks like he has eight arms, like an octopus, or a Hindu god. But most of the other hotels don't use this poster; they have designed their own posters, painted in exaggerated, hyperreal colors, in the style of Hindi film advertising. In these posters, the stars are barely recognizable as themselves and look more like Hindi film stars. Roger Moore resembles Shah Rukh Khan; Maud Adams, Madhuri Dixit.

In the movie—which we see that night, at Rajesh's insistence, my first viewing since I was a child—Lake Palace is occupied by a sexy, wealthy Englishwoman. Her father was a member of Her Majesty's Secret Service, like Bond, but she has taken a different route. She is the head of an organized crime ring, consisting of other beautiful white women, all living with her in Lake Palace. When Bond asks her where she finds so many young Western women, she says she finds them in India, wandering. She doesn't know what they are looking for, she says, but they are everywhere.

We tell Rajesh we want to see the real Rajasthan. He says OK.

We expect him to take us to some part of town where tourists never go. Or maybe to a nearby village, a *real* village, not one of the fake villages with gift shops and billboards on the highway.

Instead, he takes us to an old mansion in town that has been converted into a cultural center. We sit on the floor in a covered courtyard and watch what are billed as traditional Rajasthani classical and folk performances, though it is clear they are designed especially for tourists.

In one of the acts, marionettes engage in a salacious, pelvis-thrusting dance, which sends titters through the audience and makes me feel uncomfortable. In another, women in mirrored head coverings and ankle bells dance around a fire.

When it is time for the final act, Rajesh nudges me. His eyes widen. "Watch this."

The announcer explains that in the villages, it is the woman's job to collect water for her family. She may have to walk many miles, often over hot, desert sands. In a drought, the announcer says, she will have to walk even farther. The more she can carry in one trip, the better.

The performer emerges in a dark purple gagra choli with a large brass pot on her head. I expect someone young, but she is old. Her face is wizened. There is a drum, and she moves along with its beat, mechanically. Her eyes are foggy and far away.

After a minute or two of dancing, she makes her way to the edge of the stage, where a man standing on a raised platform adds another pot to the top of her head. The dance goes like this, every couple of minutes the man adding one or two more pots. When she is carrying six, and everyone in the audience has figured out the pattern, a new element is added. While the man on the platform is adding pots, another man is spreading something on stage for her to dance over, barefoot: one time hot coals, another time a shattered mirror, a third time nails.

Everyone in the audience oohs and ahhs as each new thing is added.

By the end of the dance, she has twelve pots on her head. There are twelve swords on stage, turned on edge, lying head-to-head in a straight line. She balances across them like a tightrope walker.

That night, Rajesh suggests we eat dinner at a place that specializes in Rajasthani thalis. It is farther into town, away from the tourist center.

Everyone there is Indian. Within a minute or two of our arrival, the waiter has already brought us our food: a large, stainless steel dish for each of us, with several compartments filled with different delicacies. We eat quickly, without talking. Everyone else is eating the same way. The restaurant has the hushed quality of a place of worship.

Any time one of us is about to finish a particular selection, the waiter instantly appears to replenish it without our having to ask.

It is our day to take Larium, and I swallow one pill and give one to Darnell.

Rajesh asks, with his mouth full, "What's that?"

I say, "It's to prevent malaria."

"Good, Sid, you are very smart, you Americans are so clever, protecting yourself, because there is so much malaria here, there are dead bodies everywhere from malaria, haven't you seen? Mother Teresa should come." There is nothing good-natured about the way he is joking. His sarcasm has a mean edge.

"Better safe than sorry," I say.

Rajesh's face hardens, even as he chews. "How can there be malaria? There isn't even water."

His anger unnerves me. I am accustomed to his being affable and docile. It is such a small thing, this minor outburst, but I suddenly realize how little I know him. I wonder, *Was this the real Rajesh all along?*

I am reminded of Carlone's cryptic comments about Rajesh as we were bicycling away from him, the day he stopped us outside his shop. *Why do you go with that boy? It isn't right.* I am worried. Just this morning I was reading in *Lonely Planet* about a scam in Agra, involving touts who lead tourists to restaurants where they are poisoned and then taken to fake doctors and charged exorbitant medical fees. Some tourists died. Perhaps a similar scam exists here. Perhaps Rajesh is in on it.

I am reminded, also, of something my mother said when I saw my parents just before my trip. My parents were both full of warnings, they who have barely visited India since emigrating forty years ago, and even then, not in years. "Be careful of bottled water. Check the caps. Buy them from reputable stores, not vendors on the street, who might find empty bottles in the trash and fill them with tap water. Don't leave your luggage unlocked. Don't go with just anyone, even if they seem friendly, even if they speak English." I rolled my eyes (though I would later heed their advice). When my mother saw my exasperation, she leaned in and said, quietly and deliberately, "Desperate people will do desperate things. You are young and lucky. You will learn."

All at once I am convinced that Rajesh is trying to poison us. I make a big show about pushing my food away. I try to signal to Darnell that he should not eat his food either, but he doesn't understand my code. It is too late. We have already eaten too much.

· · ·

The next morning, when I wake up, Darnell and I are fine. Of course. No poisoned food. Darnell is sitting on the veranda in the morning sun, reading the paper and drinking tea.

I blame my paranoia the previous night on the heat and side effects of the malaria drug, which I vow to stop taking.

I decide perhaps I am overtired. We send one of the hotel boys to tell Rajesh that we will not be meeting him today. We spend the day relaxing in our room, blasting the air conditioner, and swimming in the rooftop pool. We make friends with a young couple: a Western-raised Indian from Canada and his white girlfriend. We have seen them around, they are difficult to miss, there are not many guests.

We make fun of them behind their backs because they are trashy. We see them in the pool, midafternoon, making out, the girlfriend straddling his hips. That night, when we eat dinner together in the rooftop restaurant, she wears a tight dress with a low neckline, and a wide, gold lamé belt.

When the bill comes, the boyfriend pays for all four of us. I knew he would. Earlier, he told me about his father, who had come to Canada with very little money and little education, and had made a fortune starting stores that box things up and ship them all over the world. When the boy pays the bill, signing the charges to his hotel room, I can see in his face the pleasure and urgency of someone who is only one generation removed from having nothing.

The next morning, Carlone stops us again in the street.

"You will visit my shop today?"

"Time is short," I say. "We are leaving tomorrow."

"Tomorrow?" Carlone says. "How could that be? How is that you have not even had tea with me once?"

"We are in a rush," I say, and Darnell and I edge past him.

"You are always in a rush," he says, angrily.

We meet Rajesh at the café. He tells me he likes my pants. I have worn them before, and he has complimented me before. They look generic, but they are expensive designer pants I bought cheap at a sample sale in SoHo.

"Those pants have so many pockets." Rajesh says. "They are good for keeping paints and brushes."

Rajesh has probably noticed the frayed hem. He probably thinks I will not want to bother taking such shabby trousers back to America. I understand this is how he acquired the Diesel jeans, the leather loafers with contrast stitching.

Today is the day Rajesh is taking us to his house to look at his paintings. It is centrally located, and I wonder why we haven't been meeting there all along, instead of at the café.

It is an old stone house, one story tall, with four or five small rooms facing an open-air courtyard, and covered walkways connecting the rooms. The walls are cracked and crumbling. Nothing is painted. A scalloped archway separates the house and the courtyard from the street, which itself is only a small side lane.

As we walk past one room, he points inside and says, "Those are my sisters," but he doesn't invite us to meet them or to enter the room. From the courtyard, the room seems small and dark. His sisters are sitting on the floor, sifting lentils in front of a large, old television with dials. The reception is bad. Through the static, I recognize a song from a popular Hindi film.

We pass another room with the door shut. "That is my mother's room."

I know, without his telling me, that she is sick. I know by the closed door and the heavy silence within the room. I know by the sisters sifting lentils alone.

I also know, by a garlanded portrait hanging in the hallway, that his father is dead.

When we enter Rajesh's room, I am surprised by the mess. It is a very small room, poorly lit, like the sisters' room, with old newspapers and rags stacked in corners. There are pens and pencils and paints everywhere.

Rajesh unlocks a metal cupboard, and withdraws a cardboard portfolio. He clears a surface on the cluttered desk and opens it, spreading out the paintings. "Pick any you like," he says. "I will give you a good rate."

The paintings are just as I would have expected, just like the ones I see in the windows of every tourist shop in town: miniatures painted on silk and parchment, subjects like camel caravans, courtyard scenes, men with delicate beards relaxing under trees, smoking hookahs.

He shows us a triptych with the three palaces—City Palace, Monsoon Palace, Lake Palace—each with a different animal in front of it. He explains to us that the peacock represents beauty; the elephant, strength; the camel, love. In the painting, the lake is full. "This is my original design," he says. "You won't see it anywhere else."

Earlier that day, Darnell and I argued about whether we would buy a painting. Despite everything, I was hesitant to break my promise to myself. I said, "We have already given him so much: fancy meals he would never have been able to afford otherwise." Darnell said, "We owe him this." In the end, I agreed.

We finally settle on two portraits from the very few paintings that are not in the miniature style: a Rajasthani farm man in a red turban with a blue background and a Rajasthani woman in a yellow sari with a green background. We already have two frames at home the perfect size.

Rajesh tells us how long it took him to paint each portrait, and then he multiplies that number by an hourly rate to arrive at the price. He shows us the math, which he scribbles on the back of an envelope. Darnell and I do not haggle.

"What about the rains?" I ask Rajesh. "We still have a month of traveling. Won't the paintings get ruined in our backpacks?"

"Don't worry," he says. "I will wrap them nicely. Nothing will spoil them."

We agree to meet the next day at the café, on our way to the bus station. Rajesh will bring the package, and we will pay him.

When we leave, there is a small boy bouncing a rubber ball in the courtyard. He was not there earlier.

"My brother." Rajesh lifts him, and the boy squeals. I notice a large rip in his pants.

"So sweet. How old is he?"

"Twelve."

I am shocked. He is so small. I know very little about children, but I know this boy does not look twelve.

It is in this moment that I understand Rajesh will not attend the J.J. School of Art in Mumbai. He will not visit France. He will not move to London. He will not go anywhere.

By the time we bicycle back to the hotel, it is dark. I want to stop to buy water bottles, but Darnell needs to use the toilet, so he rides ahead.

When I reach the hotel, Carlone is in the street waiting for me. He steps directly in front of my bicycle. He grabs hold of my handlebars and catches my front wheel between his legs. His brothers surround me. They have been drinking.

"Where is your friend?"

"He is at the hotel."

"You think I am not good enough even to drink tea with?"

"That's not so. I have been busy."

"We know what you have been busy with."

His brothers laugh. Carlone is angry. His eyes are narrow and bloodshot. He sets his jaw. "Tell me: Which do you like?"

"What do you mean?"

He motions toward his brothers. "Which do you want?"

"I don't understand."

He says, through clenched teeth, "I will give you a good rate. Choose."

They have closed in on me. The night is dark, without much moonlight. During my visit, I have barely noticed the brothers, I have barely given them any thought. As I look at them now, wondering how I am going to get past them, get back to Darnell safely, something strange happens. I catch myself, for a split second, considering Carlone's proposition. Not that I ever would, but if I could, no, if I *had to*, which would I choose? I realize, looking at Carlone's puffed chest, his swagger, his desperation and unwillingness, that I wouldn't choose any of the brothers. I would choose Carlone.

"I want to go home."

I mean the hotel, but I am thinking now about my real home, how far I am from it, how far Carlone and his brothers are from theirs.

"Look, I will come to your shop tomorrow morning, I promise. We will have tea, I will look at paintings, whatever. But please, let me pass."

He says, "You had better."

The next day, Darnell and I both sleep late. Our bus isn't until afternoon, and we aren't scheduled to meet Rajesh until just before our departure.

I haven't told Darnell what happened the night before. He will worry. Whatever problem Carlone has, it is with me, not with him.

I am not sure whether I will visit Carlone in his shop, whether I will keep my promise. There is nothing he can do if I don't. In a few hours, I will have left this town for good.

Darnell and I eat a light breakfast by the rooftop pool. The young man from Canada is there. He is on his mobile phone, talking loudly to his father, who is visiting Delhi.

Darnell wants to have a swim. I tell him I'd like to take a walk, to look at the town one last time.

Even as I leave the hotel and am standing across from the shop, I am not sure I will stop to see Carlone. His brothers are outside, sitting in their plastic chairs, but Carlone is not. I could walk right by.

Instead, I stop. The brothers smirk as I pass them and enter. Carlone is sitting behind a glass counter, arranging paintings. He behaves as though nothing has happened, as if I were just any other customer, stopping in casually.

We are alone. The brothers are outside. *Guarding the door,* I think. After a few minutes, one of the brothers brings us tea from the street. I sip, even though I don't trust it. I never drink tea from street vendors. It isn't safe.

Carlone removes several paintings from beneath the glass case and spreads them out before me. They look very much like the paintings Rajesh showed us the day before. In fact, there is even one exactly like the triptych Rajesh claimed was his original design: the three animals in front of the three palaces.

I ask Carlone which of the many pieces he himself has painted. He picks out several, haphazardly, without looking.

He quotes some prices, without my asking, multiplying the time by an hourly rate which is lower than Rajesh's, scribbling down the calculations on a scrap of paper.

"I told you before, I am not going to buy."

Carlone looks at me. He puts down the pencil and pushes the scrap paper aside.

"What is he to you: Darnell?"

"He is an old school friend."

"I think he is more than your school friend."

Before leaving America, Darnell and I read in *Lonely Planet* that homosexuality is illegal in India, punishable potentially by life in prison. Other travelers told us not to worry. They said, no one is ever prosecuted, especially tourists. I consider telling Carlone the truth.

"He is a very good school friend," I finally say. My mother would approve of my discretion. *Why take chances?*

Carlone looks like he is going to say something else. I get up and start walking toward the door. I think he is going to stop me, or maybe his brothers will out front, but no one does. When I turn around, I see Carlone calmly putting away the paintings beneath the glass.

Rajesh has packaged the paintings well. They are sandwiched between cardboard, wrapped in a plastic shopping bag, and secured with several layers of clear, heavy packaging tape. The shopping bag is from a toy store that bears the name and the image of Sai Baba, a beloved prophet from the turn of the century, who has been co-opted to hawk everything from stainless steel cookware to Internet services (Sai Baba Cyber Café!).

I hand Rajesh payment in an envelope from our hotel. I have written his name in beautiful calligraphy letters. But he doesn't notice, or at least he doesn't comment on it. I had made a special effort. I had wanted him to say, "Sid, I didn't know. You are an artist, too."

He opens the envelope right away and counts the money. I have written him a note on hotel letterhead: "Thank you for your beautiful paintings and for your friendship. Good luck in the future."

"I like the way you have written this," he says. "I can show this to other tourists. They will be impressed someone staying at such a fancy hotel has bought my paintings, and then they will want to buy, too."

As he says this, he is already looking past us at some new people entering the café.

Weeks later, back in America, after having traveled through Rajasthan, Gujarat, Uttar Pradesh, after hiking to the Valley of Flowers in the Himalayas and visiting Mahatma Gandhi's ashram, after having stopped in London three days to break up the long return journey and to visit a friend, we finally open Rajesh's package, which we have been carrying in our backpacks. We carefully cut away the heavy shipping tape.

It is empty. There are no paintings. There is nothing between the cardboard.

Darnell says, "Maybe he forgot," but I can tell he doesn't believe it, even as he says it.

A few days later, Darnell remembers about the French gallery with the website, the one Rajesh said featured some of his paintings. "Maybe we can find out something about Rajesh through the website."

We can't remember the name of the gallery, but we think we'll find it if we type Rajesh's information into a search engine. We include his name, the town, the word "artist."

There is nothing about the French art gallery, but something else pops up, something called "Men of India." The link takes us directly to a profile.

The text reads:

Name: **Rajesh**
Age: **19**
Height: **175 cm**
Weight: **68 kg**
Zodiac Sign: **Taurus**
Interests: **Meeting people. Artist. Travel. Top and also bottom. Everything.**
Where to find me: **German Café or Savage Garden**

I remember Rajesh's defense of the German owner, the fat man in the silk kurta with the handsome young Indian: *He is a nice man.*

A photograph accompanies the profile. In it, Rajesh is wearing a pair of jeans, not the Diesel jeans, but another pair. This must have been before he acquired them.

He is beltless, shirtless, shoeless. He is leaning against a stone archway.

His hands are in his pockets, his arms straight and his elbows locked, so that his jeans are pushed deliberately low on his hips. The edge of his pubic hair is just visible.

He is smiling. It is an expression I have come to know: a smile that is not really a smile. He is squinting. The light is bright on his face. *Another day without rain.*

I recognize the stone archway Rajesh is leaning against. It is the archway to the courtyard of his house, viewed from the street, the one we walked through when we visited him and he showed us his paintings. Through it, somewhere in the background, out of the camera's view, are his sisters in the small, dark room with the large TV; his mother, bedridden, behind a closed door; his brother, bouncing a rubber ball, losing control of it periodically, running in and out of the frame of the photo.

I print the picture, along with the text that accompanies it, and put it in one of the frames I was saving for Rajesh's paintings. In the other frame, I put the cartoon sketch Rajesh drew in my notebook that first day. The elephant. *Strength*. I hang both on our living room wall.

Soon afterward, we are having a friend over for dinner, a woman Darnell knows from work. She notices the pictures and spends a long time looking at them, wondering, perhaps why they are so prominently displayed: an ad from the Internet and an amateurish sketch. Finally, she asks, "What are these?" "Artifacts," I say. "It's a funny story."

THREE

Citizen

Everyone told her this is what she should want, her children, her grandchildren, even her friends back in Bombay, whom her children only let her call once a month, international long-distance still being so expensive. When she told Mrs. Gupta (actually *Princess* Gupta, who lived in a lovely flat above the pricey pizza parlor on Marine Drive) that her children wanted her to take an exam to become a citizen, Mrs. Gupta clicked her tongue and said, "Ranjan, *darling*, just do what they say. At our age, what else can we do?"

Easy for Mrs. Gupta to say. She had money: enough to stay in Bombay even after her husband died. No need to burden her only child, a handsome cardiologist in Atlanta, married to a white woman, living in such a magnificent house that it was photographed by *Architectural Digest* (the son's good taste, not his wife's). So what if Mrs. Gupta had needed to rent her ground floor to a noisy pizza parlor? Three stories were too many for her. And if the noises were sometimes too loud, if the kids continued to stream in and out later and later, their coffers of black money from Mummy and Daddy deeper and deeper, well, then Mrs. Gupta could run the rumbling A/C and ceiling fans in the summer, and in the winter she could sleep with earplugs. Mrs. Gupta, Ranjan thought, had to admit her sacrifices were small.

For Ranjan Shah, things had not been so easy. Sure, she'd once had money, but her husband's untimely death (he was just forty-seven) had ushered in an era of shrinking apartments, a smaller one every few years, until she was finally living in just one room and a bath, and then, one day, when Ranjan was in her eighties, even that was more than she could afford.

So her children, a daughter and three sons, brought her to America and passed her around like a hot potato: from Cherry Hill, New Jersey, to Bethesda, Maryland, from Poughkeepsie, New York, to Wheeling, West Virginia. She spent exactly three months at each house, then it was time to board a plane or train to travel to the next. Since she spent the same three months at the same houses each year, she came to associate each one with a season. Even when she lost track of the days, she knew when it was time to switch houses by the colors of the leaves and the temperature of the air against her face.

R anjan was at her second son's house in Poughkeepsie when the World Trade Center was bombed. She was alone at home, watching the towers fall on the large, flat-panel television. She had lived through violent times—first, World War Two, then Partition—but something about seeing the destruction on such a large screen in the living room made it all seem so much more immediate and real, and she was frightened. She tried calling her son at his office, but when she lifted the receiver, she realized she had forgotten the number. She was forgetting a lot of things these days.

A few months later, her daughter, Swati, broached the subject of citizenship.

"Mummy, who knows what will happen in the next few years. Better you become a citizen. Then, no matter what happens, no one can make you leave."

Ranjan couldn't think of what could happen to make someone want to send her away.

"What does this mean, *citizen*?" Ranjan asked. Her English was not good. Her husband and children had spoken fluently, even in India, but Ranjan found she could never quite learn.

"We are all citizens here," Swati said. "All your children, grandchildren. You must become a citizen, too. You want to stay here in America with us, don't you?"

Ranjan nodded. She had nowhere else to go.

Of all her children's houses, Ranjan enjoyed Swati's best, even though she felt that it was inappropriate for a mother to live with her daughter, even for part of the year—especially with so many sons available.

Most of her grandchildren were grown: in college or off in the world making lives of their own. All her children worked, as did their spouses. Ranjan found herself alone most days in large, drafty houses with big-screen televisions, and multiple remote controls she could never remember how to work.

Once, she was blamed for spoiling a flat-panel television, the very same television on which she'd watched the towers fall. Her second son and his wife returned home one night and the picture was all snow. Her son and his wife stood in front of the television, and the wife shook her head and said, "Your mother must have done something." Much later, after they sent the television to the manufacturer, they found out the damage was caused by a power surge. No one apologized to Ranjan.

She rarely left the house, except sometimes in the early evenings when she'd wander along the streets of the subdevelopment, without fear she'd get lost, since all the streets led in circles.

In Swati's house, at least in the last couple of years, she had company. Swati's son, Pradeep, had been home. When he first finished college, he had needed somewhere to stay while he looked for a job. "A couple of months," he had said. But a couple of months turned into a year and a year into two, and now he was home a second fall with no immediate prospects of leaving.

Ranjan knew it was unbecoming for a healthy, grown man to be home all day, to not be working. She thought he must either be lazy or a little stupid. She was ashamed. But she was happy for the company.

Pradeep's Hindi was no better than his grandmother's English, much worse in fact, but they found a pidgin language in which to communicate, and what they couldn't find words for, they managed to communicate in gestures. Pradeep became so used to the pidgin language that sometimes he would forget and try to speak it with his parents or, worse, his friend, Mike, who would have to remind him, "I *do* speak English as a first language."

Ranjan told her grandson rambling stories about his family, his mother and uncles, their mischievous pasts (his mother accidentally burnt down her dorm!), even stories about her own childhood, the daughter of a diamond merchant in a remote province in the north. At first, Pradeep seemed interested in these stories. He even said one day he'd put them all in a book. This scared Ranjan and for a while afterward she stopped telling him stories. But eventually her need for human interaction overcame her sense of familial modesty.

After a while, Pradeep began to lose interest in his grandmother's stories, and eventually he stopped coming to sit beside her on the living-room sofa. Instead, he rose late and spent long afternoons in front of the computer playing video games or idly surfing the Internet, and when his grandmother came to see him and put her thin hand on his shoulder, he said in as nice a voice as he could manage, "Nani, please leave me alone. I'm working."

No one thought it would be easy for her to pass the citizenship exam, least of all Ranjan. Swati told Pradeep that he could earn his keep by helping his grandmother prepare. So eight weeks before she was scheduled to appear for the exam, Pradeep started to prep her. Her days were organized around the exam.

On the wall at the foot of her bed, Pradeep hung an American flag, large enough that it occupied most of the wall. He wanted it to be the first thing she saw when she woke and the last thing before she went to sleep. On the wall above her dresser, he taped a portrait of George W. Bush. On the other wall, he put up a poster listing all the presidents, including their pictures and names and dates of service, in writing too small for Ranjan to read, even with her glasses.

He bought her a CD-alarm clock, which he placed on the night table, and set it so that each morning at seven a.m. it would play the national anthem. It was sung by a skinny black woman Pradeep had pointed out once on the television. "This is Whitney Houston," he had said. "In America, she is a big star." Ranjan didn't like her or her singing style. Too many vocal flourishes, as though the notes were flowers and she were a butterfly unable to settle. Ranjan preferred Lata Mangeshwar, queen of Hindi film music, twice as old as the black woman on TV, and plump, not skinny, a microphone in one hand and a hill of sweetmeats in the other. Her voice was smooth, not fickle. To Ranjan, *this* was a singer, *this* was a woman.

Each morning, after Ranjan woke and had her tea from the American presidents mug Pradeep had bought her, she would watch thirty minutes of a video titled "So You Want to Be a U.S. Citizen?" Pradeep would set up the DVD for her and sit with her on the living-room sofa. The total series was six hours long, so every two weeks Pradeep would repeat the series; by the end of two months Ranjan had seen the whole series four times, some episodes even more. Still, each viewing may as well have been the first, for all Ranjan could remember. Even the next day she often couldn't recall what she had watched the day before.

She couldn't help it. Every day when Pradeep started the video, she fully intended to pay attention. She knew that her children were counting on her. But within minutes of the start of the video, after the blond hostess had introduced the day's lesson, smiling with teeth whiter than Ranjan had ever seen on a real human being, Ranjan had drifted elsewhere. Her mind had traveled oceans and decades. She wondered if she had remembered to pay the doodh wallah, if the dhobi had brought back her husband's shirts. She wondered if the cylinder had enough gas to last until Diwali or would she need to call for a new one. Had Swati remembered all her books for school and had she put her hair in plaits properly? Sometimes Ranjan would catch herself; she would try to focus on the woman with the teeth. But these English words, to Ranjan, were empty.

In the afternoons, Pradeep wanted his grandmother to practice her English. It was one of the requirements of the exam. He asked her to read aloud from the day's newspaper. Ranjan would stumble through the columns, skipping words and sentences as though the omissions made no difference to the meaning of the reports. Sometimes, when she was really struggling, she would invent whole sections, and the world became a place of creation. Pradeep, of course, instantly knew when his grandmother was improvising, because her voice would become animated and the words elementary. He usually stopped her right away and said, "Nani, read properly what's on the page." But sometimes he would let her go on. Secretly he enjoyed it, the fantastic world his grandmother created, in which everyone was fed and all conflicts ended amicably. The world she created was full of happy endings.

At night, Ranjan returned to her room and looked at the posters on the walls, the stiff American presidents with their squared-off jaws and tight collars. In her room in Bombay, Ranjan had hung garlanded pictures of Rama, Sita, and Ganesha.

In fact, her room in Swati's house could barely be called hers at all. She was in each of her rooms in each of her children's houses only a fourth of the year, and the other nine months, after she left, the rooms slowly returned to their former functions—bill paying, ironing, storage for items that belonged nowhere else—until it was time for her to return. The room where she slept in Swati's house was where Pradeep kept his weights and lifting bench when she was gone.

When Ranjan moved to another house, she had nothing to leave behind in her rooms. A lifetime of items purchased and collected and hoarded had been dispersed among living relations or sold off with her succession of shrinking flats. Now, all she owned were two suitcases, one big and one small—filled with plain cotton saris and medications prescribed by her first son or her second son's wife or Princess Gupta's handsome son in Atlanta—which followed her from house to house.

Ranjan missed the ring of jangling keys, which, for decades, had hung from her petticoat: keys for every door in every flat, every cupboard, all of which had to be locked against unscrupulous servants; even the drawers holding scrap paper and string had to be secured. When she first came to America, Ranjan would absentmindedly pat her hip and be surprised at the missing key ring. In America, cupboards didn't have locks. It made Ranjan nervous. She imagined if no one were home, the items might, of their own volition, simply float away.

The day before the exam, Pradeep brought Ranjan a gift. "For you to wear," he said, and pulled the clothes from the rustling Wal-Mart bag. He handed the dress to Ranjan and she fingered the fabric. "Denim," Pradeep said. "It's what all Americans wear. Let's see it on."

Ranjan held the dress against her body. She hadn't worn a dress since she was a small girl, since she had become old enough to wear saris. She even wore saris to bed. The dress reminded her of nothing more than the thin gowns she was asked to wear in the doctors' offices. It would make her look naked.

"Shabash!" Pradeep shouted, making an effort to use the Hindi word. "It looks great. Just the right size. Put it on."

"No, no," Ranjan said. "I am tired now. Let me wear it tomorrow only."

"OK," Pradeep said. "There's a shirt, too." He handed her a white turtleneck to wear under the dress.

"Sleep well," he said. "Tomorrow's a big day." Then he shut the door and left.

Ranjan folded the white turtleneck and put it carefully on the chair next to her bed. She didn't know if the dress should be folded or hung, and she fumbled with a hanger before folding the dress, too.

She'd taken to talking to George W. Bush the way she occasionally talked to the picture of Rama in her Bombay flat. He told her not to worry about the exam, she'd do just fine. The other presidents, from their small photos and in their small voices, concurred.

The day of the exam they had to drive all the way down to Charleston, the state capital, and they were running late. First Ranjan was embarrassed to come out of her bedroom in her denim dress. Swati finally coaxed her out and everyone had to ooh and ah over how smart she looked, how very American. Ranjan didn't know how to move in such a garment; all her motions were slowed and she kept looking at the dress and smoothing down the front.

Then, in the car, Ranjan fiddled and fussed with her seatbelt, and Swati had to count to ten slowly, like the television commercial instructed you to do to keep you from hitting your child. Ten minutes on the road, Ranjan remembered that she had forgotten her glasses, and they had to turn around. Swati told Pradeep, "I think you better take your grandmother on your own. I don't think I can handle it."

By the time they reached Charleston, there was no time to eat the teplas and drink the tea Swati had packed. Pradeep had wanted to eat them down by the river, the gold dome of the capitol building reflected in the water. He thought the scene might instill in Ranjan a sense of pride.

They stumbled through a maze of government buildings before finally finding the right office. Though they were a few minutes late, they were asked to wait almost forty-five minutes before being directed into a small room by a thin man with thick, black-framed glasses. He introduced himself as Mr. Parker. He asked them to sit in the chairs on one side of his desk, and then he sat on the other and opened a brown file and began sorting through papers.

"Well, ma'am, all your paperwork is complete," he said.

Ranjan looked questioningly at her grandson. The man followed her cue.

"Your grandmother?" Mr. Parker asked. Pradeep nodded. "All her paperwork's in order," he said again. "All she needs to do is pass the exam, which I will administer orally. She needs to answer ten questions correctly. You'll have to leave the room while I give the exam."

Ranjan had trouble understanding the man and his thick Appalachian accent. She could only catch a few words here and there. His voice was nasal. His vowels were big and unwieldy, so that Ranjan found she couldn't grab on. He sounded unlike anyone she had encountered in any of her children's houses, or anyone on TV for that matter. She longed for the blond woman with the sparkling teeth from the videos. At the time, Ranjan hadn't liked her, but at least she could somewhat understand her.

Pradeep patted his grandmother's hand and got up to leave. When he was halfway out the door, Ranjan began to whimper. "No, babu, no." She reached a bangled hand toward him.

"She's afraid," Pradeep said. "She's old. Can't I just sit with her?"

Mr. Parker considered it for a moment. The rules were clear: no other parties allowed. Still, he was not a heartless man. People liked to think of government employees as bureaucrats, insensitive and unthinking. Mr. Parker made a point to be neither. He could bend the rules when necessary.

"Fine," he said. "You can stay. But you must not say anything during the exam. She has to answer the questions by herself, without help or translation. If you try to help, I will ask you to leave or fail her."

"OK," Pradeep said.

Mr. Parker turned to Ranjan. "Before I ask you questions, I need to test your English with dictation." He handed her a blank piece of paper and a pencil. "Please write down the following sentence. I'll dictate it slowly: 'We hold these truths to be self-evident, comma . . .'" Mr. Parker paused to allow Ranjan to write the first phrase, but her pencil wasn't moving. She was looking pleadingly at her grandson. Though she had written nothing, Mr. Parker continued, "' . . . that all men are created equal, comma, that they are endowed by their Creator with certain unalienable rights, comma.'" Mr. Parker paused again, and Ranjan still wasn't writing. "' . . . that among these are life, comma, liberty, comma, and the pursuit of happiness, period.'" As Mr. Parker was finishing reading the last phrase, Pradeep whispered to his grandmother in Hindi, "Likho." *Write.*

"I'll repeat the sentence once more," Mr. Parker said. This time, when he started reading, Ranjan began scribbling. When he was finished, Mr. Parker took the paper from Ranjan, squinted at it, and showed it to Pradeep.

Ranjan had written in Hindi.

Pradeep had never fully learned the Devanagari script, but he recognized enough of the characters to realize his grandmother had written the first couple lines of the Vishnu mantra she chanted to herself morning and night.

"She's written exactly what you told her," Pradeep said to Mr. Parker, "only in Hindi. She's translated it. Actually, that's higher-level thinking than simply copying dictation, don't you think, to write 'We hold these truths' in Hindi?"

"You're not supposed to talk," Mr. Parker said. Pradeep mimed a zipper across his mouth.

"Let's move on. Mrs. Shah," he said, making an effort to speak slowly and enunciate clearly, "how many branches of government are there and what are they called?"

Ranjan looked at him blankly. She understood "branches." She thought of a banyan tree and its knotted limbs.

"Shall I repeat the question?"

Ranjan looked to her grandson.

"OK," Mr. Parker said, "let's try something a bit easier. What are the colors of the American flag?"

Ranjan heard "flag" and perked up. This one she knew. She remembered the flag on the bedroom wall. "Vite?" she said. "Red?" she said. "Good," Mr. Parker said. "One more." Ranjan was confused. She only remembered the stripes.

Such an easy question, Mr. Parker thought. Poor woman. He thought of his own mother, how, toward the end of her life, she suffered with Alzheimer's at a time when very little was known about the disease. Mr. Parker looked in the other direction as he pointed emphatically at his periwinkle necktie.

"Blue," Ranjan said, and smiled such a big smile Pradeep had to break his silence with applause. Mr. Parker smiled, too.

Ranjan understood that she had to give a total of ten correct answers. She hoped this would count as three.

"I'll give you another easy one," Mr. Parker said. "What city is the capital of the United States?"

Ranjan knew she knew the answer. So many times Pradeep

had asked her. So clearly Ranjan could remember the asking of the question; she could even see his lips forming the words. But somehow she couldn't remember the answer.

"London?" she said. Mr. Parker looked at Pradeep and Pradeep shrugged.

"Hmmm . . ." Mr. Parker said. "Let's try it this way: From which country did America win its independence in 1776?"

Ranjan was silent.

"What did you say before?" Mr. Parker asked. "Say it again."

"London?" Ranjan asked.

"Close enough," Mr. Parker said.

Pradeep clapped again. Mr. Parker laughed, and Ranjan laughed, too.

"Do you know the first line of the national anthem?" Mr. Parker asked. "Do you know the words to the song?"

Ranjan remembered the skinny black woman with her vocal flourishes. She liked Mr. Parker. She wanted to show him what proper singing sounded like. In a soft, even voice, doing her best Lata Mangeshwar, she began the first few bars of "Mujhe Kuchh Kahaa Hai" from the film *Bobby*.

Pradeep recognized the song instantly. *Bobby* was the hit movie in India around the time when Pradeep was a baby and his parents had first immigrated to America. Alone in a new country, they had played the soundtrack constantly, using an old tape deck with big reels. Pradeep didn't bother risking the no talking rule to try to convince Mr. Parker that his grandmother had translated the "Star-Spangled Banner" into Hindi. The melody sounded nothing like it.

Ranjan and Pradeep sat across from the capitol building, eating their teplas, Ranjan sprinkling masala on hers and

Pradeep dipping his in honey, and drinking tea. The legislature wasn't in session. The buildings were deserted. Fall was on its way. Ranjan could feel its beginnings in her fingers.

Swati, Ranjan's daughter, had become a citizen only eight years before. She had kept her Indian citizenship for a long time in case the family decided to go back, and even after they'd decided definitively to stay, she kept finding reasons to put off the exam. Pradeep remembered when she passed the exam, he and his father had bought her a big cake with the American flag drawn in icing, and candles that were like Fourth of July sparklers. There had been no doubt she'd pass, so they'd ordered the cake days before.

This time no one had ordered a cake for his grandmother.

Ranjan remembered what her daughter had said when she first brought up citizenship. She said if Ranjan was a citizen, no matter what, no one could make her leave.

Now, sitting on the bank of the river, Ranjan thought about how it would happen. She pictured men in suits coming to the door one afternoon when no one else was home. She wouldn't be able to remember any of her children's office phone numbers, and she wouldn't know how to ask the men to wait until evening. Or perhaps there'd be an official letter, maybe even a telegram, which would tell her—in curt, urgent, uncompromising language—that it was time to leave, and her children would shrug and say there was nothing anyone could do.

As she finished her tepla and took her last sips of tea, Ranjan thought about Princess Gupta in her flat on Marine Drive. She'd be happy to see Ranjan again. Perhaps she'd ask her to move in with her: two old women, sitting on the balcony in the evenings overlooking Chowpatty Beach and the Arabian Sea, the teenagers below them with their Western tastes: eating pizza, and, over the loudspeakers, listening to singers like the skinny black woman who had sung the national anthem.

Years ago, circumstances had forced Princess Gupta to sell off all her royal jewelry. Before she sold them, she had costume copies made of all her favorite pieces. Ranjan imagined the two of them wearing them, the costume copies—the earrings, the crowns, the diamonds and rubies and sapphires—around the house, in the kitchen, on the balcony, even in the bathroom. It would remind them both of better times. Princess Gupta would start calling Ranjan "princess," too, just for fun.

Their children would telephone, now and then. The princesses would answer the phone, if they were home, but often they wouldn't be. In which case, their servant would say, "They're out, painting the town red, as always," in such rapid-fire, colloquial Hindi that the servant would have to repeat it several times before the children could understand, and even then the servant couldn't be sure that they did. The children would just grunt, grudgingly, and hang up.

Yes, Princess Gupta would be happy that Ranjan had returned.

Ranjan felt the coolness of the approaching autumn on her face, and she looked at the oak trees across the river with their strong, straight branches.

Her grandson, who had finished packing up the picnic items in the car, stood next to her now. He took her hand, and his hand was warm. The two watched the river for a moment, the gold dome of the capitol reflected in the water.

"Chalo, Nani," he said. "It's time to go home."

FOUR   *The Better Person*

Frank is on the phone with my brother's wife, Ellison. They talk often, which surprises me because they are nothing alike. Ellison has decorated her and my brother's house with gold-framed posters of Impressionist paintings and plastic flowers in white urns from their wedding. Frank, on the other hand, pisses out the bedroom window when he's drunk. I don't worry about him hitting people on the street, because the window faces an alley. But on summer nights, when everyone's windows are open, I wonder if some of it sprinkles into the apartments below. I once asked him this, but he shrugged. In New York, he said, worse things come through your window than piss.

That makes Frank sound like a loser, but he's not. He loves me, though he wouldn't admit it. Not in those words. I wouldn't either. I don't think I've ever said "I love you," except maybe in an ironic baby voice.

But I know Frank loves me. That's why he talks to Ellison on the phone. They compare notes about me and my brother.

Ellison must have asked about me now because Frank says, "Deepu's been sulking all afternoon." He smiles at me, and I scowl back. "He always mopes on Sundays." I don't need to hear my boyfriend talking about me like I'm not there, so I take my coffee mug and pack of cigarettes and go into the living room so I can do what I do best: chain-smoke and play scratch-'n'-sniff with my body parts, while obsessing about how much I don't want to go to work tomorrow.

Though Frank and I have been going out for three years, we had no intention of moving in together. It just happened. I lost the lease on my sublet and planned to stay with him a couple of weeks until I could find a new place. Then, without warning, his roommates Jack and Carly moved out. That was three months ago. So we were stuck.

Jack and Carly took everything: the stereo, the TV, all the furniture. Frank doesn't own anything. My sublet was furnished, so I don't own much either. We look like squatters, sleeping on a filthy futon, both of us sharing one nubby gray towel. Neither of us has lifted a finger in three months. What few dishes we have—mismatched and chipped—are perpetually dirty in the sink, and we only wash them one at a time when we need them. There are spaghetti sauce stains on the linoleum floor. Dirty clothes everywhere. Soap scum in the sink and tub. I have to close my eyes when I lift the toilet bowl lid, it's so disgusting.

We haven't figured out what we are going to do in the long term. Maybe we'll stay in the apartment. Be a real couple. Buy a bed, a couch, some plants. Invite people over for dinner. Or maybe we'll decide we're not ready for all that, and I'll find a studio for myself in Brooklyn Heights with a loft-style bed so close to the ceiling I can't sit up and read, and a bathroom so small I'll have to squeeze in sideways. Or maybe we'll leave this city, one at a time or together—new apartments, new lives. Who knows? Since Jack and Carly moved out, we haven't even talked about it. The first of the month I give Frank a rent check and without a word he stuffs it, with his, into a white envelope and mails them. Each time I think to myself: *Next month . . . we'll talk about it next month.*

On my fourth or fifth cigarette, Frank finishes his phone call and comes out of the bedroom.

"There's trouble in paradise," he says.

"What do you mean?" I ask.

"Ellison and Rajiv may be splitting up," he says. "She suspects he's about to leave her."

"Rajiv didn't say anything to *me*," I say.

"I'm sure he'll call you."

Frank says he's going to take a nap. I finish my cigarette, then join him.

When Rajiv and Ellison married two years ago it was a big deal in my small town in West Virginia. It was the first Indian wedding, and my parents spared no expense. The ceremony was so lavish, the Sunday paper ran a full-color, front-page photo of Rajiv and Ellison flower-laden on the red mandap making seven circles around the wedding pyre. The caption read: *Tradition has it whoever returns to his or her seat first will be the one who controls the relationship.* The caption didn't identify who won: Ellison. Later, Rajiv told me he let her.

Rajiv rode a white horse to the ceremony, and I walked next to him, carrying an enormous square-shaped parasol over his head, red with gold bells jingling from each corner. That's not what scared the horse. My cousins did, though not on purpose. When they lit the firecrackers, the horse whinnied, reared up, and galloped into the woods. Rajiv was barely hanging on, and the trainer had to chase them and coax the horse back to the wedding hall.

When they returned, Rajiv's turban, stitched with real gold zari, was missing. We sent a search party into the woods, but no one could find it.

When Rajiv and Ellison got engaged, they had only known each other a few months. I thought it was too soon. I remember when the horse ran off with my brother, I thought, first, *Please don't let him get hurt,* and then, *Here's your chance, Rajiv: Run!*

I was bored during the ceremony, the Hindu priest droning in a dead language I couldn't understand. The twins kept stealing Rajiv's shoes, and each time he sent me after them with twenty dollars for payment. By the third time I was so irritated I didn't even pay Dilip and Meena. I snatched the shoes and pocketed the money.

Actually, there were two weddings. The day after the Hindu ceremony there was a Jewish one at a Unitarian church. It almost didn't happen because the string quartet didn't show up and Ellison sat in her dressing room crying. She said, "There has to be music when I enter." I was the one who found the girl, a distant uncle's daughter, who could play "Für Elise" from memory on the piano, stopping and stumbling when she forgot a chord. Ellison was born Protestant but had converted in college, around the same time she became a vegetarian. At the Jewish ceremony, there were exactly three Jewish people present: Ellison, the rabbi, and the ex-roommate Ellison claimed was responsible for her conversion. I didn't understand that ceremony, either. I focused on my father standing next to my brother and how strange he looked in his white satin yarmulke and morning suit, so unlike any father I knew, and my father's father, who had refused to wear the yarmulke, thinking it was a Muslim skullcap and in his old age unwilling to be convinced otherwise. It was hot that day. In all the wedding photos, my brother's hair is wet and flat against his forehead, his clothes are in disarray, there are dark stains under his arms and around his collar, and Ellison's face is streaked with sweat.

When we wake up from our nap, Frank wants to fuck. I don't. In my head I count how long it's been since we last had sex, and when I calculate it's only been three days I decide I can safely push him away without his complaining. I'm right. He lies on his side, his head propped on his arm, and looks at me, his hand gentle on my back.

Last week during one of our marathon telephone conversations, my mother asked me which one of us, me or Frank, was the woman in our relationship.

"Neither of us, obviously," I said. "That's what makes us gay."

"Very funny," my mom said. "Someone on *Oprah* said that often gay couples have one person who plays the man and the other who plays the woman. So I was wondering which you were."

"Frank and I don't believe in hetero-normative gender roles," I told her. I knew my mom didn't know what "hetero-normative" meant, so I figured she'd drop it.

"So who does the cooking and cleaning?" she asked.

I could have truthfully answered "neither of us." Instead I asked, "Is that what you think womanhood is, Mom, cooking and cleaning?"

My mom got quiet. I felt bad. I imagined her cursing herself for coming to America and raising such a disrespectful son, for letting him attend a liberal-arts college and take women's studies classes and think he knows more about womanhood than his mother. I started to apologize, but she cut me off. "It's OK," she said. "I know you didn't mean anything. I didn't either. I'm sorry for asking you those questions." Like every phone conversation I've had with my mother, she ended, "I love you."

When I was ten and my mother went back to work full-time outside the house, she stopped watching prime-time television with my dad and my brother and me. If I listened, beneath the laugh track, I could hear kitchen cabinets shutting, pots clanging, or the vacuum cleaner humming in the other room. Sometimes late at night while I tried to sleep, my bedroom directly above the kitchen, I could hear the sound of water and gold bangles clicking against ceramic plates. Early the next morning, she'd be up long before anyone else, already in the kitchen, another long day begun. Perhaps this is what my mother really meant when she asked, "Who is the woman?" She meant: *Who is the better person?*

Instead of cooking and cleaning, if my mom had asked me which one of us gets fucked up the ass, me or Frank, I would have said I do and that still doesn't make me the woman, it only makes me the *bottom*, which isn't the same thing at all. Though I had an ex-boyfriend who couldn't understand that. One morning after sex, he had held me in his arms and begged me to move in with him. Rubbing my stomach, he said, "Let's settle down; let's make babies."

After Frank and I have been lying awake in bed for several minutes, he asks me what I want to do tonight. Back when Jack and Carly were here and we had a TV, we would all watch the *The X-Files* on Sunday nights. Jack and Carly would sit together in the oversize chair, bundled up with pillows and blankets. They were always touching each other, even when they were in the kitchen or walking down the street, and it made Frank and me sick. To prove a point, we sat extra far from each other on the couch whenever they were around.

Now with no TV, Frank offers Chinese take-out and a movie, neither of which appeals to me.

"What about going out?" I ask.

"Like, *out*-out?" Frank asks.

"Let's go to a club," I say. "We haven't been dancing in forever. We only ever go to bars. I wouldn't mind sweating out some toxins."

"And ingesting some new ones?" Frank adds.

I think about it. Sunday night is a great going-out night, not too crowded, because all the bridge-and-tunnel kids have gone home and all the yuppies have to wake up early. I have to wake up early, too, but all I have to do at my job is answer phones and type and file, so it doesn't matter if I haven't slept. I remember a club on Avenue B that's trashy and fun. We used to love it there. We decide to go.

When my brother got married, I had asked my mom whether it was OK for me to bring Frank to the wedding. "You're kidding, right?" she asked. "Yes," I said, "I'm kidding," though I wasn't.

Two days after the wedding when I returned to New York, I called my brother and cried. I hadn't meant to cry. I had meant to say I had a nice time, it was good to see him, I'm happy for you. Instead, when I heard his voice I bawled. I wasn't sure why.

"It's OK," Rajiv said. "We're all having post-wedding depression." He paused, as if to consider something. "Last night

Ellison shoved a fistful of pills in her mouth. She did it right in front of me. I had to make her spit them out."

I pictured this, Ellison walking into the room, crying, her mouth stuffed with pills, one or two slipping out, glistening with spit. Then Rajiv panicking, prying her mouth open, reaching his fingers in, bending her over the toilet, and forcing her to spit them out. What did they say to each other afterward? How did they sleep?

"I'm so sorry," I told Rajiv. "Is she OK?"

"She has episodes. She doesn't know what she's doing," he said. "See, you're not the only one. We're all fuck-ups. Don't tell anyone."

That night, as I lay down to sleep, I thought of Rajiv and Ellison in their house. During the wedding, there were women in diamonds and saris singing in the front room, applying intricate mehndi designs to each other's hands, and men in gold silk breaking coconuts on the porch. But not anymore. They were gone and the house was empty. Rajiv and Ellison were alone, listening to each other breathe.

Around midnight, Frank and I take the subway to the club. I want to ask him about the apartment, what we're going to do about our future and living together. That's what I mean to say when I open my mouth. That's what I'm thinking in my head. But instead it comes out, "Do you think we should have affairs?"

"What?" Frank says.

"Do you think we should have sex with other people?" I ask.

"I know what 'affairs' means," Frank says.

I don't think he's surprised by my question. We've discussed it before, whether or not we should have an "open" relationship. Some of our friends think monogamy is unnatural, bourgeois.

Frank and I sometimes agree with them in theory, but in the three years we've been dating, neither of us has strayed.

"You mean tonight?" Frank asks. "You want to have affairs tonight?"

"Yeah, maybe."

"At the club?" he asks.

"If I remember correctly, anything goes in the back room," I say. "Of course, it wouldn't be serious. Just anonymous. Meaningless."

Frank and I have our pasts, whoring around New York. Literally. When Frank first moved here, he sometimes did it for money, getting paid as much as four hundred dollars depending on the act. I, on the other hand, never *knowingly* had sex for money. Once I went with a German guy back to his hotel and after sex, to my surprise, he gave me forty bucks. I was so offended—not because he thought I was a prostitute, but because he thought I was only worth forty bucks—that when he went to the bathroom I stole the other hundred from his wallet and left.

"I'm not sure about this," Frank says.

"Think about it," I say. And I guess he thinks, because we don't talk for the rest of the ride. We read and reread the subway ads in silence.

One cold gray weekend last fall, Ellison and Rajiv paid for me and Frank to fly down and visit them. Frank and my brother are exactly the same age, and Frank was amazed how different Rajiv's life was from his own: four-bedroom house, furniture from Ethan Allen, not the Salvation Army, no leaky faucets, no toilet handles you had to jiggle, no warped doors that didn't close. The guest bedroom we slept in was pink and everything matched exactly—the comforter, the sheets, the pillow covers, even the lampshade and curtains—like they were all bought at the same store.

The four of us took a road trip to see a bridge. Though it was overcast and had rained, the drive was beautiful. The leaves had begun to turn, and the raindrops magnified the colors. The slick bright leaves, sticking to the cars and roads, looked like patches on denim.

The bridge was famous for being the longest or highest or oldest or something. At the designated photo spot, we asked a tourist to take a photo of the four of us. Later, when I examined the picture, I thought we all looked horrible, facing this way and that, not even smiling. I was convinced that we had smiled the second after the photo had been snapped. The tourist should have waited. What a shame. The bridge in the background was perfect, its smooth arch stark against the chaotic rocks of the gorge, the river below the color of gunmetal.

The last night we were there, Ellison offered to cook dinner. Rajiv had made vegetarian lasagna the night before. She said she didn't need any help, she wanted us to relax and spend time together. "It's not often enough you two brothers get to see each other," she said.

Rajiv, Frank and I played Jenga in the living room, taking turns trying to move blocks from the center of the tower to the top without knocking it over. We played three rounds, and I lost all three. During the fourth round, I took a break and went into the kitchen for juice and asked Ellison what she was cooking.

"Thai stir-fry," she said. "Vegetables, noodles, and peanut sauce. I hope you like it."

"Oh," I said, "I'm allergic to peanuts."

"Rajiv didn't tell me you were allergic to peanuts," she said.

"It's no big deal," I said. "Since you haven't added the sauce yet, I'll have mine without."

"It won't taste right," she said. She went into the living room. "Rajiv, you didn't tell me your brother's allergic to peanuts."

"I didn't know you were making peanuts," Rajiv said, not looking up from the Jenga because he was in the middle of his turn.

"Of course you knew," she said. "I only ever buy these vegetables when I'm making this dish. You went shopping with me. You knew I was making it."

"One sec," Rajiv said, still trying to place the block on top of the tower. "Let me finish my turn."

"Fuck your turn," Ellison said, swinging her arm and knocking over the tower. The blocks crashed against the wooden table. Some fell on Rajiv. Ellison returned to the kitchen.

I looked at my brother. He collected the blocks and started restacking them.

I went into the kitchen, and Ellison was dumping not just the stir-fry but the whole wok into the garbage. She was crying. "Your brother knew I was making this tonight," she said. "He deliberately wanted to make me look like an idiot in front of you and Frank." She went into the bedroom and shut the door.

In the living room, Rajiv and Frank had started another round of Jenga. Frank looked at me, his eyebrows raised. Rajiv was concentrating. He said, without looking away, "Let's order Chinese."

Later that night, my brother came out on the porch while I was smoking. Ellison hadn't emerged from the bedroom all evening. Frank was inside watching cable.

"Can I have a drag?" my brother asked. I handed him my cigarette, and he took a long, slow drag that must have given him a head rush.

"You should have said something to Ellison," I said.

Rajiv returned my cigarette. "When Ellison and I first met," he said, "I was a mess. Really a mess. I didn't tell you and Mom and Dad because I didn't want you to worry. I was having anxiety attacks. They felt like heart attacks. The first time I had one, I thought I was dying. I even called an ambulance. But they kept happening. I'd cry all the time. I couldn't sleep in my apartment alone. Ellison was so sweet to me. She had problems, too. We took care of each other. When I look back on that time, I don't know how I would have made it without her."

"Do you still have those attacks?" I asked.

"No," he said. "I got better. But Ellison's getting worse. We have always been there for each other. So you can see why I can't 'say something,' why I can't stand up to her or talk back."

"I didn't mean you should have stood up for yourself," I said. "I meant you should have comforted her."

Rajiv was silent for a moment. "You're one to be giving relationship advice," he said. Then he asked if he could have a whole cigarette to himself. He smoked it and then left, and by the time I went inside he was asleep.

The next morning when I woke up, Rajiv had made pancakes. Ellison was smiling. They drove us to the airport, and we laughed in the car at a funny old song on the radio, and they hugged and kissed us good-bye. As I walked toward the gate, I looked back and saw them, arms around each other, waving.

At the club on Avenue B, there is a long line outside. The man standing in front of us is wearing fake fur and sunglasses and sputtering into a silver cell phone. His backpack is shaped like an alligator, and the green sequins glitter in the light from the streetlamp.

Inside, I realize I have forgotten how to dance. I have a couple of drinks and try to relearn by watching people around me. I imitate the way one man's arm windshield-wipes the air. I imitate a bald man who throws his head around as though he has a great quantity of hair and he is making patterns, like a gymnast with a ribbon.

Frank goes to get more drinks. A boy rubs up against me and I rub back. He is cute. I lean against him, following the way his body moves. He is very young, six or seven years younger than I am, too young to be here. His thin face and wrists and long eyelashes remind me of myself when I was his age.

It's happening. I can tell it's happening, and there is nothing I can do to stop it. I tug on his shirt and pull him off the dance floor. I take him toward the back room. Frank is there with our drinks. He is with a man, and the man's hand is on his back. They are entering the back room, too. Frank sees me. He is still looking at me, when I say to the boy, "Let's go somewhere else," and we turn and leave.

Outside, we walk past a couple of buildings. I push the boy into an alley. I don't look at him anymore. I don't kiss him or stroke his cock through his jeans. I turn the boy around, push him against the brick wall, yank down his jeans. I roll on a condom I got from the safe-sex people in the club, and I start fucking him. I don't prep his asshole with my fingers. I know it hurts. I know from experience and from the tightness of his ass and the way he doesn't grunt or moan but cries. I want this to be over. I want to be home with Frank, asleep.

Afterward, I ask the boy if he's OK and he says yes. I'm sorry, I say, I'm really, really sorry. I tell him I'm going inside and he says OK. I find Frank sitting on a couch alone. The man who was with him in the back room is gone. I ask Frank if he's ready and he says yes and we get a cab.

Back at the apartment, the first thing I need is a shower. I hope I'll feel better after. When I get out, Frank is in his boxer shorts standing with the fridge door open, staring blankly into the empty fridge. In the dark kitchen, the light of the fridge makes Frank's pale skin moonlike. He shuts the fridge door and in the grayness of early morning says to me, "We didn't do anything—me and that guy in the club—nothing happened."

"Really?" I say. "I'm surprised. How come?"

He shrugs.

I briefly consider whether I have to tell Frank about the boy in the alley.

After a minute, I say, "Something happened with me."

"I know," Frank says. I think he is going to say something else, but he doesn't and he goes into the bedroom.

I can't stay here. It's only a couple of hours until work. I decide to go to a diner, get some breakfast, have coffee. I pick the least dirty clothes up off the floor, put them on, and leave.

For the first Monday in all the Mondays of my adult life, I am happy to be at work. I am thankful for the fluorescent lights, the empty conversations, dress shirts and slacks. Even the filing. I am thankful I can see the order in things.

By six o'clock, most of my co-workers have left. I want to leave, too, but I can't face Frank. He's bartending tonight, but he won't leave home until later. I decide to call my brother.

"How you doing?" I say, happy that Rajiv has answered and not Ellison.

"I've been better," he says.

"Ellison told Frank," I say. "You know ... that you guys are having problems. And Frank told me."

There is a long pause. He's not ready to talk, I think. I should have waited for him to call me. I cough so that he knows I'm still there.

"Am I a terrible person?" Rajiv asks.

"No," I say. "Of course you're not."

And then I ask him the question I have been waiting to ask since Frank and I visited last fall: "Why did you get married?"

If I had asked him two years ago, before they married, why they were doing it, my brother would have said, "We're in love; we want to spend the rest of our lives together," and to everyone, maybe even me, that would have been enough.

Now he answers, "We needed each other."

Then he says, "I called Dad and Mom on their anniversary this year. I talked to Dad while Mom was in the shower. Do you know what I asked him? I asked him if he was always in love with Mom, if he was *still* in love with her. He hesitated and then he answered, 'Of course, my family is my whole world.' He didn't say he was *in love* with *Mom*."

"That's what he meant," I say, but I know Rajiv isn't satisfied. "Mom and Dad had an arranged marriage," I remind him. "They hadn't even met each other when they got married. The phrase 'in love' doesn't mean the same thing to them as it does to you."

"Dad hesitated," Rajiv says. "When I asked him the question, he hesitated before he answered. That means something."

"It doesn't mean anything," I say. "You didn't see his face. You only talked to him on the phone."

"In thirty years," Rajiv says, "when someone asks me if I'm still in love with my wife I want to be able to answer right away, 'Hell, yes!' In fact, I want it to be so clear that no one would even think to ask me."

"No one would ask you because it's a rude thing to ask," I say. "What kind of son asks his father that?"

Rajiv says, "You don't understand. I don't want to be Dad."

I don't want to talk anymore. "I have to go," I say, and hang up.

Shortly after my brother got married, my parents insisted that he and Ellison travel to India together. Many of our relatives missed the wedding because they were unable to obtain visas or they couldn't afford the airfare. "It's not right that they haven't met her," my father had said. "You should go, too," my mother had said to me. "It's been ages since you've visited India. We'll pay." Frank was jealous. He'd always wanted to go to India. I promised to call often and to take lots of pictures.

When we visited the village where my parents were from, the village where my grandparents and many of my relatives still lived, there were whispers among family members about a distant cousin in Bombay (so distant, we weren't even planning to see him) whose wife had recently left him. Apparently, she had disappeared so suddenly that she had abandoned, along with her husband, a closet full of clothes and shoes. "Such expensive beaded heels!" I'd heard my grandmother hiss.

If there was, in my relatives' native language, a word for divorce, it wasn't used by them. Instead, the word was always spoken in English, even when the rest of the sentence wasn't. In their minds, divorce was a Western concept and the English word should be used. They'd pronounce it with a long "i" and with emphasis on the first syllable: *DIE-vorce*. A divorce wasn't neutral. It wasn't a mutual decision. Someone *gave* it. "She gave the DIE-vorce." Someone had failed. Someone was to blame.

"She's ruined," an uncle had said, "a complete outcast. Who will have her now?"

Listening to my relatives' hushed conversations, I wondered whether there was, in their language, a word for homosexuality. I doubted it. I doubted, even, that the English word was used. For them, the concept was unspeakable.

When I finally leave work and go home, Frank is gone. The apartment smells like Pine-Sol. The floor is mopped, the toilet scrubbed, the clothes washed and folded. The kitchen sink is empty, the dishes stacked in the cupboard. The apartment feels strange and new.

Taped to the fridge is a note: "You'll probably be asleep by the time I get home," it says. "We should talk soon."

Walking around the clean, empty apartment, I have images of a red chair here, a floor lamp there, a poster on that wall. This apartment could be someone's home. Maybe someone else's, a couple more like Jack and Carly, holding hands in the kitchen, clinging to one another on the couch. Or maybe a couple like us.

I'm exhausted. It's been almost two days since I've slept. In the bedroom, I remove my clothes, careful to fold them and stack them neatly in the corner. I pull back the comforter on the futon. There are fresh sheets, I realize, as I climb in.

FIVE *Ten Thousand Years*

W hen I told Thomas about my experience—"transcendent" I called it—he was skeptical. I had only been studying yoga for three weeks. Thomas, on the other hand, had been practicing yoga and meditation for eight years. In all that time, he hadn't felt anything even close to what I was describing.

I told him maybe I had an edge, being an Indian and currently in India.

We were on the phone, but I had originally mentioned the experience to him in a greeting card. Here's what I described: I was on a city bus, traveling from Opera House to Breach Candy. I had just been to class at Kaivalya Dam—the same place my father had studied, reluctantly, half a century earlier, because a doctor had prescribed yoga to his mother, and she'd refused to go alone. The bus was loud and crowded, so, to escape, I decided to practice the meditation techniques I had learned in class. I chanted my mantra silently. I followed my breath. I closed my outer eyes and opened my inner ones.

That's when I transcended. My proof? I was supposed to alight near Parsi General Hospital, where I was meeting an old family friend. Instead I ended up at a shopping mall in Bandra hours later with an overwhelming sense of contentment and no memory of how I'd gotten there.

On the phone, I could tell Thomas was avoiding giving any reaction to my story. When I pressed him, he said, "I'm not sure it was what you think it was."

"What do you mean?"

"Sunil," he said, "are you sure you didn't just fall asleep?"

"I know what I felt," I said. "You don't believe me?"

"It's not that. It's just that, as you deepen your practice, you'll understand how naïve your claim sounds."

Naïve. I remembered the card I had sent him: A sheep on the front dabbed at its tears with a Kleenex wedged in its hoof. Inside it said, "I miss ewe." I thought he'd think it was funny.

"Someday," he said, "you'll reread what you wrote and laugh."

"How will I reread it?" I asked. "Haven't you thrown it in the trash?"

The previous fall, a few days after Thomas's birthday, I'd found the birthday card I had given him in the wastebasket by his bed. When I asked him how it had gotten there, he said something about "avoiding clutter" and "just because I don't keep things doesn't mean they mean any less to me." I reminded him now of that conversation.

"I'll keep this one," he said. "I'll show it to you when I visit in May."

"Keep this up, and you may want to consider canceling."

I had come to Bombay three months earlier, leaving Thomas, my boyfriend of less than a year, in New York. Parting was difficult. He brought me to the airport, accompanied me through the long line at the Air India counter, kissed me good-bye before I made my way toward security. I told him I would return as soon as I could, though I wasn't sure when that would be. Thomas promised to visit.

My parents thought that, as the eldest grandson, I had come to Bombay to take care of my grandmother, since all her children lived in America, and she was increasingly unwell. I thought I had come mostly to learn Hindi and its close cousin Marathi, so I could translate some little-known eighteenth-century Indian poetry and finally finish my dissertation. Thomas thought I had come because I didn't know what I wanted—in life or in love— and it was easier to run away than stay and sort it out.

As for my grandmother, I wasn't sure what she thought. She looked at me suspiciously. Late at night, I could hear her rummaging in cupboards she kept locked. I was living with her in the same flat in which my father had grown up, on the third story of a well-appointed building in Breach Candy. She had windows facing the sea and marble floors everywhere, but she had let the place deteriorate since her husband had died. The couch in the living room had lost its legs and was now fit only for dwarfs. The drapes were dingy. She couldn't bother shooing the crows that flew in the window, so she let them come and go as they pleased. They hopped on her kitchen counters, picking at lentils and taking chapatis to go.

Worst of all, when I picked up the phone upon my arrival, I found the line dead. In my grandmother's bedroom, I discovered a desk drawer full of unopened bills.

At the telephone office the next day, none of the clerks spoke English, and my Hindi failed me. We honked at each other and flapped our wings but got nowhere. A few days later, my grandmother's upstairs neighbor intervened on our behalf. Afterward he said to me, "It could be weeks—maybe months. Who knows? This is *India*."

So I would make my calls to America from one of the expensive international pay phones scattered about the neighborhood. I had two nearby from which to choose. One was attached to an open-air tobacco stand abutting a busy boulevard and lacked the benefit of even a booth to dampen the sounds of scooters and cars. Men hung around it in a cloud of smoke and exhaust fumes, bidis pinched between their fingers. Some chewed betel nut; their red spit stained the sidewalk like paint splatters.

I preferred the phone at the laundry across the street. The shiny, heavily air-conditioned shop catered to a wealthy clientele. The shopkeeper was pleasant and always wore a clean white shirt with a Western collar. But even here, privacy was a problem. The small phone, an urgent red, was on the same counter across which business was conducted. As I talked, customers would come and go, looking at me curiously as they waited for their clothes or change. The phone was wired to a digital readout that hung on the wall, displaying the charges as they accrued at an alarming rate. The shopkeeper, when he wasn't busy, would listen to my conversations, chin in hands, elbows propped on counter, eyes on the red numbers as they raced higher. I thought he'd be thrilled by his profits, but he looked concerned, perhaps wondering if this would be the time I couldn't pay. He appeared relieved only when my money was in his palm. Then he slapped me on the shoulder and shook my hand vigorously.

As I entered and exited the store, two raggedy boys loitering on a low stone wall tried to sell me American products I didn't want: one day a package of Schick disposable razors, another day a travel-size bottle of Shower to Shower deodorant powder. They held the items in their small fists, which opened before me like dirty lilies.

Once, one of the boys showed me a single Marlboro menthol. I said, "I don't smoke."

He looked baffled and said sternly, "You should."

Not long after my conversation with Thomas about my "transcendent" experience, I phoned him from the laundry. After we'd discussed our mutual friends in New York, my grandmother's idiosyncrasies, and Thomas's impending visit to India ("You will see things that will haunt you for the rest of your life," I said, refusing to elaborate), Thomas told me unceremoniously that he had cheated. At first I thought *taxes*. Then I understood.

"I'm so, so sorry," he said. "I love you."

In some ways, I wasn't surprised. We'd promised to try to be faithful to one another while I was away, but I'm not sure either of us really believed it.

"How did it happen?" I asked, not sure I wanted to know.

"I meant to go straight home after yoga, but I had overdone it. My body ached. I stopped for a beer."

"Where?"

"The Works."

I knew the bar. I had been there once, before I'd met Thomas. That night I had gone home with a stranger—tall, muscled, blond—who would realize the next morning, in the stark fluorescent light of his building's elevator, that I wasn't cute enough for him. His realization would be so visceral, so obvious that, upon reaching the lobby, I would know without having to be told that we would not eat brunch as planned, would not linger alfresco over eggs Florentine and mimosas, would not exchange phone numbers or promises to call. I pictured Thomas with such a man, but because Thomas is much more handsome than I am, the outcome in the elevator would be different.

"What did he look like?" I asked.

"What does it matter?"

"It matters to me."

"This isn't going to help," Thomas said. When I didn't respond, he said, reluctantly, "Medium build. Average height. Nice smile."

"Was he cuter than me?"

"No."

Before, I hadn't been sure I wanted to know the details. Now I couldn't seem to stop. "What did the two of you do? Did you do the things we do? Or did you do something new?"

"I was lonely," he said. "I miss you so much. I only wanted to be touched."

"Did you suck his dick?"

I looked at the shop owner, who was looking straight at me and biting a hangnail. His English was good, but how good? Did he know *dick*? Did he know *suck*?

"What did it look like?" I said more quietly.

"I don't remember."

Thomas probably thought his lack of attention to detail would prove to me that the incident had meant nothing, that he hadn't lingered. Instead, it made me think that he didn't notice anything, not even what was right in front of him.

"I'm the one who got hurt," I said. "You owe me at least this. What did his dick look like? Big, small? Hooded, cut? Thin, thick?"

Thomas sighed. We were both silent.

After a moment, he said, "Bent."

I hung up on him.

Much later, walking along the rocky seashore toward Mahalaxmi Race Track, fixating not on Thomas's infidelity but, more specifically, on how Thomas had described the man's dick, I thought, *Like a finger, beckoning.*

I waited a week and a half before calling him back. I had meant to say something funny—perhaps "How's my little adulterer doing?" I had hoped we could laugh and move on. Instead I started crying and couldn't stop.

Thomas stuttered syllables that sounded like "Sorry"; I interrupted him with sobs. The laundry man watched the numbers on the digital display shoot upward. I watched, too. Finally, after a very long time, I hung up. I paid the laundry man one thousand rupees—about thirty dollars, a small fortune.

He asked me if I wanted my clothes now. I said I did, and he said, "Thirty rupees," and I gave him that, too. He brought me my bundle, and I left.

Outside, the boys stared at me as I walked past them. They must have seen I had been crying, was still crying. One of them offered to sell me a saltshaker shaped like the Empire State Building, and I waved it away.

Thomas arrived in Bombay a few weeks later, as originally planned, except a day late, and in the morning instead of at night. There had been a delay in Kuwait, and he and the other passengers had spent the night in a hotel. Thomas was cranky because the officials had confiscated the bottle of Grey Goose vodka he had brought for my grandmother. I'd told him she would like it, even though she didn't drink, because foreign liquor was a status symbol, and she could serve it to guests. The officials hadn't returned the bottle, although they had promised they would.

I said to him right away I wasn't sure this was going to work. We were in a taxi, driving through the slums that surrounded the airport. "Maybe I shouldn't have let you come."

"I would have come anyway," he said, smiling. He pulled at my earlobe, and I brushed his hand away.

At my grandmother's flat, Thomas sat on the dwarf couch, drinking tea and looking small. My grandmother hovered above him, patting the key ring hanging from her waist, the one that unlocked the cupboards. Thomas wanted to sleep, but I convinced him he'd get over his jet lag more quickly if he stayed awake until bedtime. I suggested we take a walk to a nearby temple. I had been translating a poem about the temple at Walkeshwar and its famous Banganga water tank, but I had never visited, even though it was only a short distance away.

As we walked, Thomas asked about the poem.

I told him it was about the origins of the water, based on a famous tale from the Ramayana about Rama's quest to find his beloved Sita, who had been abducted by the demon Ravana. Along the way Rama stopped at Walkeshwar. He had been traveling for years and was tired and thirsty, but he couldn't find anything to drink. So Rama shot an arrow into the ground, and the holy river Ganga spurted forth.

"Speaking of tired and thirsty," Thomas said, "I think I'm getting heatstroke. Shoot me an arrow, will ya?"

"The reason the poem is remarkable," I said, "is that the poet argues that Ravana gets a bad rap in the Ramayana. He points out that Ravana held Sita captive for many years, but he never violated her, even though he could have. Ravana is actually a model of masculinity, because he protected Sita in a way that Rama, who let her get abducted, couldn't. In the poet's opinion, Ravana should be honored in the pantheon of gods, not demons."

"I'm not sure that *not* raping someone you've kidnapped is reason for canonization," Thomas said.

"You're missing the point," I said. "He restrained himself despite his desires."

"What are you trying to say?"

"All I'm saying is I'm saying," I said.

During our walk, we collected a group of street children, who stuck to our legs like burrs. They begged, "Chocolate? Pen?" I had heard this request many times from street children, usually after they'd given up asking for money. I found the pen part confusing. It was obvious to me why they would want chocolate, but why a pen? Was I to believe that this was the reason, the *only* reason, they were on the street instead of in school: lack of school supplies?

By the time we'd reached the temple and sat down by the water tank, we were surrounded. Thomas wilted. The children pulled at his sleeve until he fished around in his day pack and handed out three blue Paper Mates. When they weren't satisfied, he found a roll of cough drops and gave them out, one by one.

"That's medicine, not candy," I said.

"It's all I've got."

There wasn't enough for everyone, and one small child, who arrived too late, threw a tantrum. He pouted and wiped a soiled hand across Thomas's chest and spat at him and started crying.

"It serves you right," I told Thomas. "Do you think you are helping by giving kids who have nothing cough drops? You were just trying to make yourself feel better."

"Why are you being so mean to me?" He looked down at the brown smear across his chest, lifted his shirt to his face, and sniffed. His nose crinkled. "This is shit."

He took his shirt off and threw it away. We left immediately, walking back under the hot sun without having had a look at what we had come to see.

I hoped, after Walkeshwar, that Thomas's visit would improve. It didn't. We quarreled constantly and slept in separate beds, Thomas on a trundle, which, during the day, nested in mine: our beds intimate in ways we were not. He developed a vague, Victorian-style illness that left him feeling tired and numb. He lost his appetite for everything except oranges, which were expensive and hard to find.

I blamed Bombay. "It's the air."

I suggested we head south: first the mountains ("We might see tigers!"), then the beach. "South India is like a different country," I said. "People there don't even speak Hindi. We can *both* be foreigners."

"Do you think your grandmother will be OK alone?"

"She'll be fine," I said, ignoring the fact that her ailments had gotten much worse since I had been in Bombay.

"Maybe a relative can stay with her while we are gone," he said. I shrugged.

Thomas had taken an interest in her. He filled her hot-water bottles and bought her a silk shawl at the market. The shawl was too vivid a red for a widow (I'd told him so at the time), but my grandmother wore it anyway. She'd grown to trust him. Once, she even asked him to help her get something from one of the mysterious cupboards she always kept locked. I asked him later what was in there, but he wouldn't tell me. "If she had wanted you to know," he said, smiling, "she would have shown you herself."

Before we left Bombay, we visited a used bookstore and bought a Malayalam phrase book, choosing the only one small enough to fit in a pocket. We didn't look at it very closely until we were on the airplane.

The book was copyrighted 1967. The cover showed a cartoon drawing of a tall, blond man with long hair and bellbottoms talking to a small brown man wearing a sarong and washing an elephant. Other illustrations in the book were similar. They all showed Indian men and women in traditional garb doing hard labor—pulling rickshaws, serving meals, scrubbing floors—with Westerners towering above them. We were horrified.

The text in the book was even worse. It was filled with phrases like "That's the boy's job," "Tell the boy to come in the morning," "There is plenty of work for the boy," "Can't the boy work any faster?" "This room is filthy!" We vowed to throw it out when we arrived. But during our first day at a small hotel in the mountains, we recanted. Our room *was* filthy, there *was* plenty of work for the boy, though we didn't have the courage to say so.

One morning, eating breakfast on our terrace, we made the mistake of giving a monkey a mango. The next day he returned with three of his friends. When we refused to feed them, too, they made loud noises and hurled rocks and dirt at us. We huddled inside until the boy came and chased them away with his broom.

Things were better at the beach. We splurged on an upscale resort and a room with an ocean view.

The resort was staffed, exclusively it seemed, by beautiful boys—about a dozen of them in their late teens or early twenties, from all over India. They paraded before us like pageant contestants: Miss Orissa, Miss Bihar, Miss Rajasthan.

Our favorite was Miss Andhra Pradesh. He walked around bare-chested in a sarong, like an illustration from our phrase book. The sarong came to his ankles, but if he needed to do a bit of hard work—like hauling a bucket of water or climbing a tree to fetch a coconut (a trick the hotel management actually encouraged guests to request)—he could, with one graceful movement, halve the garment to his knees. His thin, flat torso glistened with sweat, reflecting sunlight like a mirror. Thomas and I were dazzled.

We took yoga classes at a nearby school: I, a beginning class; Thomas, an advanced one. In the evenings we practiced yoga on the beach and watched the sun set over the ocean: a spectacle that, as East Coast boys, neither of us was accustomed to seeing. We were seduced by the sight of water on fire. Later, we fed each other Cadbury squares under the night sky.

In New York, Thomas had a knack for spotting stars: uptown, Ethan Hawke waiting for the A train, scratching his goatee; downtown, Holly Hunter inhaling a slice at Two Boots to Go-Go. I never saw them until Thomas pointed them out—evidence, perhaps, that it was I, not he, who didn't notice what was right in front of me. Now, on the beach in Kerala, Thomas spotted different stars: Orion, the string of lights encircling his waist; Sirius at his side; stubborn Taurus, forever on the run.

One night, walking home along the beach, Thomas stopped me under a palm tree and kissed me long and hard. I caressed his cheek. Suddenly Thomas pulled away, and his eyes darted sideways. I heard what had stolen his attention: short, quick breaths coming from behind a nearby tree. At first we thought someone was hurt. After staring for some time, we made out the shadowy figures of Miss Andhra Pradesh giving Miss Orissa a hand job.

The next morning, while serving us breakfast, Miss Andhra Pradesh said, "Yoga is hard." He must have been watching us practice.

"It just takes getting used to," Thomas said.

The boy twisted his arms and legs like a pretzel and screwed up his face in mock anguish. "I could never get used to this."

"There are other poses," Thomas said. "For instance, sava-sana: corpse pose. All you have to do is lie still like you're dead. It's not so hard."

Thomas reached for a plate of idlis and his hand accidentally brushed against the boy's arm. The boy smiled.

That afternoon at the beach, Thomas and I practiced the headstand pose, which I had just learned that morning. I had trouble staying up even for a second and kept tumbling into the sand. Meanwhile, Thomas was serene in the pose.

I crouched in front of him and said to his upside-down face, "You think you're good? Listen to what Ravana did."

I told him the story. Ravana wanted Shiva to forgive him for all the bad things he had done, including kidnapping Sita, but Shiva wouldn't. So Ravana stood on his head for a thousand years. When Shiva still refused to forgive him, Ravana, to prove his seriousness, chopped off his own head. Luckily, he had nine more. He stood on each head for a thousand years, chopping them off, one by one. Only after ten thousand years, when Ravana was about to chop off his last head, did Shiva finally agree to forgive him.

"But it was a trick," I said. "Ravana wasn't really sorry. Or if he was, he wasn't sorry enough. Despite his promises, he never changed."

"Don't tell me," Thomas said, still standing on his head, "all you're saying is you're saying, right? But weren't you the one defending Ravana just the other day?"

I shrugged. "Demons are complicated. They can be both good and bad." I pushed Thomas over.

That night, when it was time to go to bed, Thomas said he was restless and was going for a walk on the beach. When he came back, I asked, "What took you so long?"

"It hasn't been so long," Thomas said.

I tried to sleep but couldn't. I heard Thomas breathing beside me. I imagined him, on his walk, coming across Miss Andhra Pradesh. The boy would have been leaning against a tree, his sarong flat against his thighs in the night breeze. I imagined Thomas spotting him and approaching. "Want that yoga lesson now?"

I thought of a poem I had been translating, which described the goddess Kali straddling Lord Shiva's dead body. Kali was fierce—a string of severed heads around her neck, her blood-stained tongue exposed, machete drawn—as she lowered herself upon Shiva's dead, but erect, penis. Miraculously, the sexual act breathed life back into him.

I imagined Thomas and Miss Andhra Pradesh taking turns practicing corpse pose in the sand.

.   .   .

We returned to Bombay to find my grandmother's health worse than ever. She refused to get out of bed except to use the toilet or take a bath, and even then she required help. The doctor said there wasn't anything specifically wrong with her. She was just old and tired, and her body was giving out. She could persist for several years like this, or she could go tomorrow. At her age, the doctor said, a person who no longer wanted to live could essentially will herself to die.

My grandmother called for help often, and Thomas answered her calls more often than I; he was leaving in a week and wanted to help while he could. He must have sensed I was feeling overwhelmed by the prospect of months of difficult caregiving. When he saw me feeling frustrated, he would send me on long walks. "Don't worry," he'd say. "I'm here."

He had formed a connection with my grandmother that somehow I never had. I remembered a story he had told me about how his own grandmother, whom he had loved, had fallen ill while he was in college. It had been during finals week, and he had promised to see her when his exams were over, but she'd died too soon. Perhaps he was doing for my grandmother what he'd been unable to do for his own.

My grandmother appreciated the attention. I noticed in particular that she seemed to need to be touched. She would offer any excuse. One time she complained about her earrings, large diamonds that had been part of her dowry. She said they were weighing her down. When Thomas went to remove them, his fingers brushed her ear, and I saw electricity travel up and down her body and light up her eyes. She handed him the key to the cupboard to deposit the diamonds for safekeeping. Another time she took his hand, placed it on her forehead, and asked if she felt feverish. When he said no and tried to withdraw his hand, she said, "Leave it longer, to be sure." Thomas rested his hand on her forehead, gently stroking it until she fell asleep.

On Thomas's last night in India—after we had brushed our teeth and checked on my grandmother, and after Thomas had asked once again if I was sure I didn't want him to extend his visit to help, and I'd said, yes, I was sure—I crawled into his trundle bed, kissed his ear, and whispered, "Thank you." I continued kissing him, down his neck, across to the tender hollow between his collarbones, down his chest and torso. He shimmied his hips as I slid his shorts from his waist. I started to take his cock in my mouth. He moaned. Suddenly I stopped and pulled away. Thomas sat up. "What's wrong?"

"That's the boy's job," I said.

"What?"

"That's the boy's job. That's Miss Andhra Pradesh's job."

"What are you talking about? Wait, what do you think happened?"

"There's plenty of work for the boy."

Thomas stood up, pulled his shorts on, and walked to the other end of the room, where there was a chair. "You're crazy," he said. "Nothing happened between us. I swear."

I remembered the words from the phrase book, and said them in Malayalam.

"Can't the boy work any faster?"

"I'm really sorry about what I did in New York," Thomas said. "Really. I fucked up. But can't we at least talk about this like mature adults?"

"This room is filthy!"

"Remember, you were the one who left."

"Filthy!"

The next morning, as Thomas was finishing packing, my grandmother called us to her room. She was lying in bed. She said, "My heart is weak." She pulled aside the thin sari cloth covering her torso. "Feel." She was blouseless; her breasts were stretched and scarred. I recoiled.

Thomas took my hand with both of his and placed my palm on my grandmother's bare chest, holding it there. She breathed deeply. I tried to look her in the eyes, but I couldn't. A moment later, Thomas released me. I found my grandmother's red shawl draped over a chair, wrapped it around her, and left. I finished packing Thomas's suitcase for him, while he sat by her side.

On the way to the airport, Thomas asked if we could talk about what had happened the night before in the trundle bed, and I said no.

Several minutes later, he asked what I had meant when I'd warned him, before he came, that he would see things in India that would haunt him for the rest of his life.

"Haven't you seen things?" I asked.

"Yes," he said, "but I want to know what *you* meant."

The week before that conversation with Thomas—the same conversation in which he'd told me he had cheated—I had been walking in Colaba in South Bombay. I was looking for a shop that sold carved wooden boxes. I turned onto a side street and stumbled across a woman lying in the middle of the sidewalk, completely naked. She was almost unrecognizable as a woman. Her skin was flaking, black, and charred, as if burned. Her eyes were white and wide open. Her right index finger was hooked between her legs, massaging her clitoris vigorously, violently. Passersby stepped around her, barely looking at all. No one stopped except me. She watched me watch her for a moment, her eyes wild, her finger furious, her face tensed as if with pain. Soon the passersby were glaring at me, as though it were I and not she who was crazy: crazy for stopping, for not turning away; crazy for having the audacity to look straight at what was there.

"Nothing," I told Thomas. "I didn't mean anything."

When I returned from the airport, I found the card I had written Thomas, the one with the sheep with the Kleenex wedged in its hoof. Thomas had left it on my pillow. I read it before I went to bed. He was right, of course. I did sound naïve. I *was* naïve.

In the days that followed, my grandmother kept asking for Thomas, wondering again and again where he had gone, unable or unwilling to remember. Not long after that, she died.

I telephoned my parents. My grandmother's phone still hadn't been connected, so I had to call from the laundry. I told them to come right away.

Outside, one of the boys from the wall approached me and tried to sell me a packet of Lipton instant chicken-noodle soup. When I refused, he said, "Go back to America," and returned to his friend.

The other boy shouted, "Go home! Your boyfriend's pregnant!" The boys gave each other high fives.

The funeral was a traditional affair. My father and I and the other men in our family shaved our heads and carried her body through the streets. The burden was heavy, and I realized how accustomed I had become in India to having other people do the hard work for me.

According to tradition, we dropped coins periodically along

our route. The street dwellers eagerly swept them up behind us. Our female relatives met us at a designated site by the sea. We rested my grandmother's body across a pile of logs. My father said a prayer and lay a torch upon her.

My parents and I spent the next few days sorting through my grandmother's things, preparing the flat to be sold. Her locked cupboards, it turned out, held nothing special, odds and ends from her life—old clothes, scraps of paper, years' worth of greeting cards. I found a toy car I remembered losing when I was ten—a sleek silver Aston Martin identical to the one James Bond drove. It had been my favorite. I collected the car, along with other items that seemed of marginal value, in a Benzer shopping bag, which I eventually delivered to the boys outside the laundry.

The night before my parents were to return to America, my father said it was strange sleeping in his childhood flat. He hadn't been there in years. He regretted not having spent more time with his mother before she died. He squeezed my hand and said he was glad I had been there, that she hadn't been alone in the end.

I thought of my grandmother's last days and how tenderly Thomas had cared for her when he visited. And I remembered one of the excuses Thomas had given for cheating: he'd only wanted to be touched.

I stayed in India a while longer—a year and a half total—relocating to Juhu. I abandoned my dissertation and took a job writing dialogue for a music-video show. The co-hosts were a slick Indian American named J.J., who spoke American-style slang, and a puppet named Dharmendra, who spoke only rudimentary English with an Indian village accent. Part of the joke was that they were always misunderstanding one another. They argued about everything, including which music videos to play next. Each furrowed his eyebrows when the other spoke.

When I returned to New York, I tried calling Thomas, but his phone had been disconnected.

I ran into his friend Steve at a party. He told me Thomas had returned to India months before to do an intensive, two-year-long yoga training at an ashram in Pune, not far from Bombay. He hadn't tried to contact me.

I kept up with my yoga, taking classes at a yoga center on Lafayette. I sat for meditation regularly and practiced the poses. Stillness was a struggle. My mind was a monkey.

But I had made headway with the headstand. I could get into the pose and even hold it. I was up to two minutes. I thought of Ravana, standing on each of his heads for a thousand years, trying to convince Shiva he was sorry, even if he wasn't sure he was. I pictured Thomas doing the same pose at his ashram in India. I imagined the two of us, simultaneously inverted, on opposite ends of the world.

SIX

The Cure

I told the doctor over the phone I needed an appointment fast—tomorrow, if possible. Are you going to hurt yourself, she asked, or someone else? No, I said. I was burning money. She said, Tomorrow at three, and I asked, Do you take check or credit card, because obviously I can't carry around cash, ha ha, but she didn't seem to get the joke.

I was at my best friend Yvonne's house when I called. I had gone over there holding a yellow saucepan with the charred edges of three twenty-dollar bills. Yvonne was having dinner with her ex-girlfriend Juliette and another friend, Serena. When I asked what I should do, all three said, Therapy!, and began bickering over whose therapist was best, offering me their cell-phone numbers. I was surprised their therapists were so forthcoming with their private numbers, though perhaps they had cell phones especially for work. In the end, I chose the one who returned my call first: Juliette's.

When I met with the therapist and, in the context of a memory, mentioned Yvonne, her eyes lit up and she said, Wait, you know Yvonne, too? I could see her mind working. I suspected that, as Juliette's therapist for years, she was far more interested in the drama between Yvonne and Juliette than she would ever be in me.

She asked what my job was. I said I wrote brochure copy that tricked welfare recipients into forgoing their government subsidies for an inferior managed-care plan. So you don't like your job? she asked. No, I said. My boss was impossible: she eschewed compound sentences, preferred sans-serif fonts, and had no respect for the semicolon.

It wasn't until halfway through our session that she realized the burning of money was real, not figurative. Her face turned serious and she said, We need to address your ascetic concerns. Hearing *aesthetic*, I inspected my loafers and rubbed away the outline of a raindrop.

At the end of the hour, as I was leaving, she said that in college she used to be a socialist, some would even say a radical.

I paid her ninety dollars—the lowest level on a sliding scale. I felt cheated. The money would have been better burned.

The first time it happened, I had been with Yvonne and our friends Angel and Charlotte. We were walking along a deserted block in Astoria on our way to a Greek restaurant, talking about money and power and greed. It's sad, I said. After all, money's just paper, and Angel said, mockingly, Yeah, just paper, and I said, I'll prove it, and pulled out a twenty and lit a match. There was a wind, so we had to huddle against a wall and I had to try several times before I could get it to burn. Yvonne called me a show-off and said my politics were a mess, but I think she was moved because, that night, she paid for my dinner.

Much later, she told me the fire in my eyes had scared her.

It had been the only time I'd done it in public. The other times had been alone in my apartment, burning bills over the kitchen sink or a pot or pan, sometimes one after another until my wallet was empty and I felt full.

Had it not been for Angel's goading, I probably wouldn't have started. Now, I couldn't stop.

The therapist wanted to talk about my parents. I told her that they didn't have anything to do with this. The therapist said, You're wrong. It's always about the parents.

I had a bouquet of balloons that day that said "We'll Miss You" and "Good Luck." The therapist asked about them, and I told her they were from people at work because I was quitting. She said, It's obvious you are loved, and then she smiled.

She asked if I had a new job, and I said, Yes, writing book-jacket copy for self-help books.

She said she had written a book and gave me a copy, a manifesto of sorts, advocating drug-free psychiatric treatment. She said talking could actually change the chemical composition of your brain. I told her, no offense, but I wouldn't read it, I just didn't have time. She said, Take it anyway, I have extras.

Meanwhile, the practical side of my condition was getting complicated. I had given all my cash and my ATM card to Yvonne for safekeeping, and I had withdrawn from the bank eighty dollars' worth of one-dollar Sacajawea coins that clinked around in my backpack and otherwise burdened me.

The therapist said I had a compulsion and needed something else to occupy my time. She suggested a jigsaw puzzle, or knitting if I knew how.

I went to Kidding Around and looked in the puzzle section, but nothing caught my eye. Nearby was a section for model cars and airplanes. The most complicated was a 1930s Mercedes-Benz Roadster, with almost six hundred pieces of precut cardboard and an engine that ran on rubber bands. I wanted something more plebeian, but the pickings were slim. Toy companies didn't seem interested in manufacturing scale models of Geo Metros.

It reminded me of when I was a kid and my uncle, visiting from Bombay, took me and my sister to the hobby store without our mother and told us we could have anything we wanted and I picked out a five-dollar snap-together model Toyota pickup truck and my sister chose a ninety-dollar remote-control Ford Cobra exactly like the one Cheryl Ladd drove on *Charlie's Angels* and my mom got mad and grounded my sister for choosing such an expensive gift.

I guess the therapist was right about the parents.

One morning, I told the therapist I thought I had discovered the trigger for my episodes. Here's what I said.

A few months ago I was in a village in Rajasthan, and I had to get to the bus station three miles away. A rickshaw driver offered to take me, but the price seemed too high, so I set out on my own with my luggage. After a couple of minutes of following me and watching me struggle, a young boy, maybe eight, took my bags from me and pointed to himself and the bags and then toward the bus station. I said, OK, twenty rupees, and, not seeming to know to ask for more, he nodded OK.

He balanced the heavy bags on his head and walked barefoot along the hot road under the midday sun. I offered him water, which he accepted, and he said, in English, Tank you. He called me sahib, and I said, No, I am Indian, too. But the boy didn't know English, and, armed with no Indian languages, I was helpless to make him understand.

When we reached the station, the boy was deflated. I worried that the weight of the luggage had stunted his growth. I thought, Shouldn't he be in school? In the end, out of guilt, I paid him double—forty rupees—less than one dollar U.S.

On the bus, looking out the window, not wanting to remember what the boy had called me but not being able to help it, I thought, He's wrong, I am no one's master, though secretly, at that moment and even months later, I worried I was.

A few weeks later, back in New York, my friend's mother treated me and her daughter and her daughter's husband to dinner at Le Bernardin to celebrate her daughter's birthday. The mother's face was so heavily moisturized, when I kissed her hello her skin gave way like pudding. We ordered caviar with crème fraîche. We ordered two good bottles of wine—a red and a white—and, for dessert, a sixty-year-old port. The bill was over a thousand dollars.

It wasn't long after that I burned my first twenty.

The therapist thought this was all very interesting, but my problems were more deep-seated than that. She said, In Gestalt therapy, we treat the whole person, not just the symptoms. There are no easy answers, she said. It's going to take a while.

I persisted another month before telling her I had to end it. I'm moving on Friday, I said. Wisconsin. I thought you just started a new job, she said. Oh, I said, that isn't working out.

Nothing was.

By that point, I had stopped burning money, but only because Yvonne still had my cash and ATM card and I had learned to live on plastic. I'd finished building the Mercedes-Benz Roadster. I used all the parts, and it looked all right, but I couldn't get the motor to work. I thought about displaying it, but it didn't go with my furniture.

Not long after quitting therapy, I ran into the doctor at Barneys. I was returning a belt for a friend who couldn't return it himself because when he bought it he had fucked the salesclerk in the dressing room.

The therapist knew I had lied about moving to Wisconsin. She didn't care. She was fingering an oversize purse with a rhinoceros horn for a handle.

Yvonne asked me, instead of burning the money, why didn't I send it to poor kids in India. I thought about it for a minute. I said, Money can't cure the problems it creates, though, of course, I understood it was more complicated than that. Yes, she said, sighing, but whom are you helping by burning it? I didn't respond. I knew the answer.

I thought about what the therapist had said about it always being about the parents. When my father came to America he was seventeen and had no money and few material possessions. For forty years he and my mother had worked hard and lived carefully. It's an immigrant cliché but, in their case, true. Recently, he called me, stammering, not quite knowing how to say the family's savings had swelled to seven digits.

We're millionaires, he whispered excitedly.

I tried to think of this whenever I felt like burning money, how hurt my father would be if he knew.

Eventually, the urge left me altogether. I pasted all the corners of the twenty-dollar bills, which I had been saving all along, into a picture frame with letters I cut out of fashion magazines and arranged to spell: I am not what I own. After a while, I got bored of looking at it and felt embarrassed by the bumpersticker sentiment and put something over it: a posed portrait of me and my parents and my sister at my sister's wedding to a man she had quickly divorced. He's not in the portrait. Someone had had the foresight to take one without him.

The wedding had cost forty thousand dollars. The marriage lasted less than a year.

When my sister comes to visit, she tells me she doesn't like the photo, even with her ex-husband absent. It reminds her of worse times. Worse for her, though not necessarily for me. I like the photo. In it, we all look so happy and clean.

SEVEN   *What We Mean*

Mind the deer, dear.

This is the note my boyfriend leaves me a week before he leaves me. We are both writers and clever with words. I am more clever than he is. When his *dear john* letter comes it is full of clichés.

Carson means it. Not the *dear john* letter; the *mind the deer, dear* one. I am a terrible driver, and the road I travel is famous for errant deer. A co-worker—already on probation with her insurance company for having had three accidents (all no-fault) in as many years—struck one. She is still in the hospital recovering, and her car insurance has been canceled. I believe my boyfriend is genuinely concerned for me, and that to him I am, if nothing else, at least dear.

The *dear john* letter, on the other hand, he doesn't mean. I am certain of that. What he means is meaner and more true.

We meet eight years earlier at a Halloween party in Park Slope. I go with my friend Jeff, who knows no one but the hostess, and I know no one but Jeff.

Jeff is six feet four; he is the Jolly Green Giant. I am Peter Pan.

The hostess is busy, and Jeff and I hover by the drinks. Carson looks lost and introduces himself. His costume confuses us. A clover? A pool table? Moss?

He says, "I am a lawn." He wears a sign that says, "Keep Off!"

He asks Jeff what he is supposed to be, and Jeff tells him. Carson turns to me and says, "That must make you Sprout," referring to the giant's diminutive sidekick. I don't correct him.

We continue to talk, and after a while Jeff says, "It's not easy being green," and we all agree.

We clump together like three wet leaves by a river. We drink too much. Carson is funny and sad, and I like him for it.

Toward the end of the night, after Jeff realizes we want to be alone and excuses himself early, I tell Carson I want to bury myself in him. He removes his sign and asks, "Front yard or back?"

I say, "I don't care." I whisper in his ear, "Plant me."

Within a few months, we decide to move in together, as much out of economic necessity as anything else. Rents are outrageous. We find a place in Brooklyn that is still cheap.

Around the same time, my friend Sangeeta decides she has had it with New York. She is going to try San Francisco. Her last night, Carson and I help her with some last-minute packing.

She offers us a 31" TV, which she hasn't managed to sell, but just as we're leaving, someone who has seen an ad in the paper calls. So Sangeeta gives us a hanging fern, which her landlord had given her six years before when she first moved in. He told her it needed a lot of love. "Promise you'll love it," she says.

She never named it, so Carson and I decide to call it "Krishna" because of its bluish fronds, which we think are beautiful, though Sangeeta says it may mean he's sick.

The three of us take the subway back to our new apartment, where Carson and I are going to cook Sangeeta a farewell dinner. While we are waiting for the train, Carson holds the plant up to the subway light. Turning it around, he says, "Look how beautiful you are!" He says to us, "Isn't he the most beautiful plant you've ever seen?"

Carson holds the plant in front of him by its hanger and starts spinning around, saying, "Whee!" The fern's fronds splay out. Together they look like a carnival ride.

I say, "Be careful. You're so rough. You'll hurt him."

Sangeeta sings, "Carson is the father and Parag is the mother."

I have been helping her pack almost every day for a week, and last night, tired and grateful and a bit delirious, she thanked me profusely and told me, "If Carson and you are still together, and when the time is right and I am settled in my life and you are settled in yours and everyone is happy, I will give you a baby." I wasn't sure I wanted a baby. I might have preferred a gift certificate to Bloomingdale's. Remembering it's the thought that counts, I told her thanks. Sangeeta said it didn't matter which one of us donated the sperm, but she recommended Carson, since he is white and she is Indian, like me. That way, the baby would look more like the one Carson and I would have if we could make one on our own. "Plus," she said, "halfies are so pretty."

I haven't mentioned any of this to Carson.

When Carson stops spinning, he is dizzy and looks like he might fall over. I take him by the shoulders, and I cover his mouth with mine. I think this will steady him. Instead, it makes him swoon.

A week before, in our new neighborhood, just one subway stop away, we were chased down the block by some boys from the barrio shouting, "Faggots! We're going to kill you faggots!"

They didn't catch us, though they easily could have. I was wearing clogs.

Now, waiting for the train, holding Krishna between us, Carson and I kiss, oblivious of the boys. We are scared of them. But we understand they have fears of their own.

In the coming months, the neighborhood will change. The bodegas will be replaced by boutiques and bistros. Rents will rise. The boys from the barrio will be priced out of the neighborhood. Not long after, we will, too.

After a couple of years of living together in Brooklyn, we meet a painter from out of town, who tells us lofts in Troy are cheap. We are tired of the starving part of being starving artists. So we move, not realizing that upstate we will continue to starve, just in different ways. Still, for the first time in our lives we own cars, live in a house with an upstairs and downstairs, end the month with a little left over. And we still write, though after a while our new starvation starves that, too.

Carson, who has always done odd jobs, becomes a baker's apprentice. He goes to work very early in the morning, before I wake up, and returns home a little after noon. When I come home from my job, there are muffins on the kitchen counter (seconds from the bakery, misshapen and crumbly). Upstairs, he is lying in bed, smelling like yeast.

I am an office assistant, which was my job in New York and the work I have done my entire post-college life, which isn't so long. I am not very good at it.

Part of the reason I am bad at my job is that I am fundamentally opposed to multitasking. I have been reading the Vietnamese monk Thich Nhat Hahn, who says that to be happy you must do one thing at a time. He says, do the dishes to do the dishes, not to have them done. The goal isn't to have clean dishes in the cupboards; it is to be present in the moment, to feel the water on your hands, the smooth surfaces of the ceramic bowl as you caress it. Doing the dishes shouldn't be a chore, he says, it should be a joy.

He says, think of washing the bowl as bathing a baby. Treat everything you touch as though it were a baby: with attention and care.

I try to apply this principle to my most dreaded task at work: photocopying. I try *caring* about the things I copy. I imagine the leaves of paper as little babies I feed through the Xerox machine. And the papers the machine delivers on the other side are babies, too. They proliferate in ever-increasing quantities: ten, twenty, fifty, a hundred, five hundred. I place the copies in people's mailboxes so that they can find them later, when they finish their afternoon meetings or the next morning when they check their mail. Surprise! There's a baby in your mailbox! The mailroom, where the Xerox machine is housed, is full of babies of all different colors—lavender, cherry, orange, chartreuse—sliding in and out of the copy machine, peeking out of mail slots, crying because they have been left on the counter or need to be changed.

So many babies.

I start avoiding the mailroom. My boss finds other ways to get her copying done. I am not worried about losing my job. We are more or less resigned to one another, which I am beginning to think is the way most relationships work.

Carson thinks I am crazy.
I can't disagree.

I have a habit of calling him from work in the afternoon, when I know he will be home from the bakery trying to sleep. It is bad enough that I wake him, but to make matters worse, I often have nothing to say. I only want to hear his voice. And since I have nothing to say, I meow. In the silence, I listen to him breathe. I meow for a full minute, maybe two. Then I hang up.

The co-worker who sits in the cubicle next to mine once poked his head in and said, "Is there a little pussycat in here?" He is large, in body and voice; he looks and sounds like a bulldog.

I scowl at him.

Soon we develop an unspoken understanding that we will pretend we cannot hear each other's private conversations. In truth, the walls are so thin we can hear everything: the sound of papers shuffling from inbox to outbox, chair wheels scooting across the carpet, rubber bands straining to keep things together. We nod our heads amiably when we pass each other in the hallway and joke when we intersect in the restroom, as though he does not know I meow into the telephone, and I do not know that he is cheating on his wife.

In the same way, we pretend we cannot hear the staff accountant, whose cubicle is on the other side of ours, and with whom we both share a wall. Her four-year-old son is fighting leukemia, and between clicks of her calculator and computer keyboard, we can hear her cry. When we visit her in her cubicle, we are careful not to say, "How is your son?" because if the news were good we would already know. But rather, we say, "Wan-Chen, would you please cut this check, and mail it to the address listed on the W–9 form?" We do this not because we don't care, but because we know numbers are safe and knowable; we see how they comfort and numb her.

I make bizarre grocery lists. I replace cereal with surreal, Glad bags with sad bags, coffee with sneezy, lettuce with let's. The words stray further and further from what is really meant. My lists become so coded that Carson, pulling them off the fridge on the way to the store, cannot read them. He returns with shopping bags full of wrong products.

He shows me the list, and says, pointing, "How can anyone understand this?"

I shrug. No one can. There are days even I can't.

Our house shares a driveway with the house next door. Our neighbor's boyfriend, who visits his girlfriend frequently but doesn't live with her, often parks his car in such a way that it blocks mine. Never Carson's, only mine.

In the morning, after Carson has already left for the bakery, I walk across the lawn, knock on the neighbor's door, and ask to speak with her boyfriend. I say to him, "I'm so sorry to bother you, but I need to go to work. Could you please move your car?" The first few times I am polite and gracious, but as time goes on I become more and more annoyed with the daily nuisance. I become shorter in my words and tone: "Move your car, please." I get tired of looking at them—my neighbor, whose name I can't remember, with her stub nose and chewed nails, and her unemployed boyfriend, with the gut and the crazy eyes, both of them still in their pajamas, angry at me for waking them—so, if I notice his car in the driveway the night before, I knock on her door and slip a note in the letter slot saying, "Neighbor's boyfriend: please move your car." Then, rethinking my tone and not wanting to be so curt, I replace "please" with "s'il vous plaît." Sometimes I print it on my computer using fancy fonts and graphics, and sometimes, in addition to putting the notes in the letter slot, I put them on his car, under the wipers and taped to the driver's side window: "Move your car, s'il vous plaît." And because I think *s'il vous plaît* sounds a little like *Sylvia Plath*, I change it to, "Move your car, Sylvia Plath." No one is listening to me, so why waste words? I shorten it even further to simply, "Sylvia Plath." Finally, the notes devolve into a single exclamation, duplicated a hundred times, in the mail slot, taped to the car, under the windshield wipers: "Sylvia! Sylvia! Sylvia! Sylvia! Sylvia!"

Carson sees the signs and says, "What the hell are you doing? What must the neighbors think?" I say, "The neighbors don't care. At least I'm amused."

One morning I wake up and Carson has left his car keys on the kitchen counter with a note:

Sylvia dear, for God's sake, use mine. Love, Ted.

From then on, Carson lets me use his car, while he takes the bus to work.

I think it's sweet. I am grateful for the sacrifice, even feel a little guilty, but not too guilty, because Carson's bus ride to work is much shorter than mine would be.

But I wonder about Carson's note. Had he forgotten that Ted Hughes was no martyr; that he was not a faithful husband, would not have signed a letter "love" and meant it; that, after

Sylvia's suicide, women picketed his poetry readings, claiming murder? Perhaps Carson confused him with Leonard Woolf.

One day, after returning from the grocery store frustrated, a particularly cryptic grocery list in hand, Carson asks me why I act this way, why I play these games with words.

I can't think of an answer right away. I say, "You're a writer, you tell me."

Several days later, we are fighting about little pieces of chopped onion that have spilled and stuck to the linoleum floor.

I tell him, "I cannot bear the things I must say, day after day, and the words I must use to say them."

Our last summer together, we take a trip with our friends from New York, as we do every summer, to Carson's family's summer house, called The Camp. The house was built over a hundred years ago, before the Brice family lost all its money. Most of the family's other properties were sold off long ago, but The Camp is protected by a trust.

When we are shopping for summer reading before our trip, Carson buys a recent issue of a literary quarterly that published one of his short stories, years ago, although its editors have rejected all his subsequent submissions. The recent issue is guest-edited by a woman who wrote a famous memoir about a sexual relationship she had with her estranged half-brother after they were both adults. The issue is called "The End of Love" and is filled with stories about couples breaking up.

Carson is into symbolism. During the trip, I hardly see him actually reading the quarterly, but he carries it around and places it next to him, face up, when he sits on the couch. He lies on the beach, hugging it.

This year, one of our old friends, Becky, has brought along a new girlfriend, Laura, whom none of us likes. Becky is a writer and Laura is an artist. At the beginning of every month, Laura presents Becky with a blank book she has made by hand. At the end of the month, Becky returns the book to Laura, full of poems. They have been doing this every month for the seven months they have been dating.

I think it's a bad idea.

In the car on our way to the beach, I ask Becky and Laura, "What happens when a month goes by and no one feels like making a book? Or what if someone has a busy month at work or falls ill? Or what if someone runs out of inspiration and has nothing to write about?" To emphasize my point, I start singing "You Don't Bring Me Flowers Anymore."

Becky looks at Laura and says, "That won't happen."

"But what if it does?" I ask.

Becky says, "It won't."

"But what if it does?"

Laura says, "Even if it does, maybe it would be for the best. At least there'd be a sign that there is a problem. There is nothing worse than stumbling along, with everyone knowing the relationship is over except you."

The beach where we are driving used to be owned by the Brice family. It's about two miles long, crescent-shaped, with rock jetties bracketing it on either side. Most of it was sold, fifty years ago, to the state of Connecticut, which turned it into a very popular public beach. But the family kept a sliver of sand, forty yards or so, partly to remind themselves of better times, and partly so that they would still have something to call Brice Beach, which has such a nice ring.

Neither the family nor the state erected any marker to separate the public from the private, so naturally, the crowds spill over onto Brice Beach. Usually, it isn't a problem.

On this particular day, a noisy motorboat drops its anchor just offshore in the private part. The driver, who has a deep tan, which will surely turn cancerous, is lying in his boat with the motor running. Now and then he pops up, as though he is expecting someone, and then lies back down. The motor spews fumes, chopping the water, and preventing us from swimming.

Monique, who is Carson's oldest friend, says, "Carson, maybe you should tell that guy to leave. It's your beach."

Carson is lying on a blanket with his sunglasses on, the quarterly resting open, page-down, on his chest.

"Yeah, Carson," I say. "Tell him."

Carson says nothing. Monique may have been joking, but I am getting angry.

"You're not going to tell him, are you?" I ask. I walk over to where he is lying, and my shuffling feet kick sand on him. "That's just like you. You want to tell him, everyone wants you to tell him, but you can't."

Carson says, "If you feel so strongly, why don't you say something?"

He brushes the sand off his arms and legs and rolls onto his stomach.

When Carson gets up much later, he has marks on his torso where the edges of the quarterly have dug into his flesh.

Carson finally manages to leave me the following fall. I come home and find the *dear john* letter taped to the mirror in the upstairs bathroom. I read it once standing at the bathroom sink, from beginning to end. Then I close the toilet seat cover, sit down, and read it again.

He says he needs time.

He says nothing is definite.

He says he misses New York more than he knew.

He says he is going back to sort things out. He will be at Monique's, but please don't call; he will be in touch when he is ready.

He says it isn't me.

The letter is all lies, especially the last part. If it were true, if it isn't me, then why didn't he leave the note somewhere else: on the kitchen counter, where the muffins should be, or taped to the screen of the television set, the one we bought when Sangeeta didn't give us hers? Why did he leave it in the bathroom for me to read and have nothing to look at except myself in the mirror? Why has he left me alone?

I say alone, but I suppose I am not. Krishna is downstairs, thriving quietly. We have kept our promise. He is twice the size as when we got him, and his bluish hue has disappeared. Sangeeta was right about what the color meant.

Three weeks after the *dear john* letter, a month after the *mind the deer, dear* one, the animal I encounter in the road is not a deer, but a dog. He has a plastic trick-or-treat basket, shaped like a jack-o'-lantern, stuck on his head. He is stumbling around in the middle of the road.

Several cars in front of me swerve. I pull to the side of the road and get out, intending to remove the basket, but I can't catch the dog. He is scared. There is no reasoning with him.

I decide the dog must belong to someone in the neighborhood, and I start ringing doorbells. The first two doors go unanswered; behind the third is a man who has not brushed his teeth. He looks at the dog through squinty eyes, thinks for a minute, and says the dog belongs to the woman in 152. He points down the street and quickly shuts the door.

I walk two houses down and ring the bell. A woman answers. She is wearing nice slacks and a thin leather belt and drinking a breakfast shake from a can.

"Is that your dog?" I ask.

She looks at it as though she's never seen it before. After a minute she says, "How'd that get there?" She marches out to the street, grabs the handle of the trick-or-treat basket, and leads the dog back to the door. She asks me to hold her breakfast shake. She pushes the dog into the house, without removing the basket, and shuts the door behind him. She reclaims her breakfast shake from me and says, "I'm late." She gets in her car, which is parked in the driveway.

I am late now, too, but I am worried about the dog. Perhaps there is someone inside the house to help him, though I wonder if that someone isn't the one who put the basket on his head in the first place.

I walk over to the woman and knock on her car window. She is fumbling for cigarettes. She looks startled and annoyed. I motion for her to roll down her window, which she does.

"Do you need help getting the jack-o'-lantern off the dog's head?" I ask.

She pauses and then says, "Mind your own business." She rolls up her window and adjusts her rearview mirror.

As she is doing this, I notice in her rear window a high school parking sticker that identifies her as "FACULTY." A smudge on the window obscures the letter "C."

I understand, and I forgive her her faults.

I knock on her door and motion for her to roll down her window again. "What now?" she asks.

"Every day after work," I tell her, "when I get in my car, I have to readjust my rearview mirror. For a while, I wondered why this was happening. I thought maybe someone was breaking into my car and taking it for a joy ride. Then I realized, it is because I shrink during the day. My life makes me shrink.

"I sit at a computer all day. I took an ergonomics workshop so I could figure out how not to shrink. 'Your head is a balloon,' they told me. They said, 'To correct your posture, think of your head as a helium-filled balloon, pulling your spine upward.'"

The woman's eyes have wandered to her front yard, where her dog, who has somehow gotten out of the house again, is stumbling around. He still has the basket stuck on his head.

"So the ergonomics people," I continue, "installed software on my computer, so that every forty-five minutes a stick figure of a man sitting in a chair appears on my screen. The figure's head is a balloon. The balloon makes his neck long and his spine straight. It's supposed to remind me to do the same.

"But if I were the stick figure, I wouldn't want the balloon just to straighten my spine. I would want it to carry me away, off the screen, as far away as it could."

"Why are you telling me all this?" the woman says, looking angry.

"Because," I say, "I am faulty, too."

"I don't have time for this," she says. She shifts the car in reverse and peels out of the driveway, almost running over my foot.

I look at the dog, who is whimpering and pawing at the basket on his head.

I try again to remove the basket. Now he is too tired and defeated to resist. When I get it off, he licks me.

It is no longer early morning. My boss will already be at work, as will my co-workers. Wan-Chen will be crying quietly at her desk, since mornings are hardest for her.

I have decided what to do. I will rescue the dog, which I have already, in my head, named "Lucky." I will put him in the car, turn around, and drive home.

But when I bring the car over and open the passenger door, Lucky doesn't want to get in. He looks at me and runs in the opposite direction. He dashes around the front yard, toward and away from the house, barking insistently. He sounds strange, not like a real dog, but more like a cartoon dog, or a stuffed dog with a speaker and a button that says, PRESS HERE.

What is he barking at? It could be anything: the sun, the tree, a squirrel or a bird he has glimpsed out of the corner of his eye. Or maybe he is barking at the small blue house itself. Or someone inside the house, or something that has happened there. How can anyone know what happens in houses?

I think of TV dogs like Lassie, Benji, and Rin Tin Tin. When those dogs bark, they are trying to communicate something vital. People who hear them understand. Someone is trapped in a burning house. Someone is tied to a chair in an abandoned warehouse by the wharf. Someone is holding on to a branch in a fast-flowing river heading for a waterfall, and the branch is about to break.

EIGHT

Yours

1.

When Antwon was awarded an Individual Artist Grant from the NEA—back when the NEA was still routinely awarding such grants; before Congress, enraged by artists like Andres Serrano submerging a crucifix in a vat of piss and Karen Finley smearing her naked body with chocolate, threatened to defund it—Antwon used the money to hire men for sex and then write about it.

Don was one of them. Or so it would seem.

That was before Don was my boyfriend.

Don wasn't a prostitute. He was Antwon's friend. He was also his former student: "Structured Improvisation," at a summer dance festival a few years earlier. Don was still in college then. Now he was in New York, trying to make his way in the dance world.

Antwon knew Don needed money. Don knew Antwon wanted him.

Antwon was almost twice his age. (Not that he needed to pay for sex: he had a dancer's body.)

Even after Don and I met and moved in together—a one-bedroom in Crown Heights overrun by cockroaches we named after conservative politicians—Don continued to see Antwon once every couple of weeks. They sat at a back table at Kiev, and Antwon ate pierogies and Don, borscht. Or they met on a Monday night at Marion's and drank cosmopolitans.

I knew what they ate, what they drank, because these were answers to questions I allowed myself to ask.

One of Antwon's short stories about paying men for sex is anthologized in a collection of gay erotica I discovered on my bookshelf shortly after Don and I moved in together. I found the book on a shelf I had designated for Don. We segregated our books on my insistence. I told him that, as a writer, I needed to be able to locate my books with ease. Don was suspicious; he detected no order—not alphabetical, not even thematic. The truth was, I didn't trust the relationship. It was all so new. I was already imagining the night we split up, the following days: looking for new apartments, untangling our lives. I remembered the scene in *St. Elmo's Fire* after Ally Sheedy and Judd Nelson have broken up. For me it was the saddest part of the movie. They are sorting through records, unable to remember which belongs to whom, fighting over an artist they both love. As a concession, Judd Nelson says, "You can have all the *Carly Simon*," sneering at the singer's name. In our case, Don and I would fight over the Carver; Don would say to me, "You can have all the *Anne Tyler*."

In Antwon's short story, the narrator asks of the young man something simple, but specific. He wants to enter him from behind, something the young man has never allowed anyone to do. In the story, the young man is hesitant, and he takes a few days to think about it. When he finally agrees, saying, "I need the money," Antwon's narrator isn't surprised by the rationale (after all, he's heard the young man express his need for money on many occasions). However, Antwon's narrator can't help pointing out the irony, the obvious falseness, of "this white boy" (those are the narrator's words), a recent graduate of an Ivy League school which he attended as a fourth-generation legacy, selling his body because he "needs the money." "Surely," Antwon's narrator notes, "*need* means something different to him than to me."

I was lying on the floor in the apartment, still reading Antwon's story, when Don came home.

"It's not about me," he said, without my asking.

Several months earlier, when Don and I were drunk—slumped on the cheap leather couch at the Boiler Room, The Smiths' "How Soon Is Now?" on the jukebox, the white stuffing from the ripped couch glowing in the black light along with the white of Don's eyes, into which I was looking—I had asked Don, "Who is Antwon?" and Don told me about Antwon's project paying men for sex. I knew this short story in this anthology was an account of Don's participation. The hair color might be different, the eyes, the name, but I could recognize Don in a story. There are things only a lover knows.

"It isn't me," Don said again. Out of the corner of my eye, I caught Rudy Giuliani skittering under the dresser.

I was still holding the book, and I pointed to the dedication in italics just below the title: *To Don, for Inspiration.*

"I don't believe you."

2.

One night, about a year after I found the book, Don said to me, "Antwon asked me to ask you if you want to participate in a reading he's curating." Don told me the name of the reading series, which was prestigious and which I myself had attended many times. I was flattered but unsure.

"He's never read my work. He doesn't know anything about me."

"Antwon is lazy. He's probably filling the program with friends."

"I'm not a friend," I said.

I told Don to tell Antwon I'd think about it.

A week later, Don came home from drinks with Antwon (Temple Bar: martinis) and handed me a stack of cards with a note: *Please distribute.* The card announced the reading, and it listed my name along with three others'.

"I never said I'd do it."

"You're stuck now."

I thought: *Antwon has a way of getting what he wants.*

I only had one story that seemed polished enough to read. It was called "The Night Jagdish Learned to Drive." In it, the sixteen-year-old narrator, Jagdish, is woken by his mother late at night. She tells him her father—his grandfather—is gravely ill, and they are all driving from West Virginia to Chicago in a matter of hours, and she is hopping on the first flight she can get to Bombay. She hands him a list, and asks him to drive to the twenty-four-hour supermarket to buy what she'll need: toilet paper, deodorant, tampons. She either forgets or chooses to ignore the fact that Jagdish has only a learner's permit and is not allowed to drive at night, not even accompanied by an adult and certainly not alone. While at the store, he buys, in addition to the items his mother has requested, a porn magazine. He pulls to the back of the parking lot and, under the dim lamps, studies the pages, focusing on a pictorial story of a couple named Rocco and Lacey. It's Lacey's birthday, and she's at a bar all alone. At closing time, Rocco, the bartender, tends to her birthday needs. Jagdish tucks the magazine away. But later that night, while he and his parents are driving to Chicago, Jagdish finds himself replaying the images from the magazine. He remembers Rocco in particular, and Jagdish furtively masturbates in the backseat, while his parents are in the front, his father driving. The next morning, not long after daybreak, Jagdish's father tells him he is exhausted. Jagdish takes over, and the story ends with an image of him at the wheel.

Later, in a writing workshop, a classmate would rip apart the story—"Isn't 'driving' too obvious a metaphor for Jagdish's sexual awakening? Didn't someone else just publish a story using the same metaphor?"—and I'd find myself agreeing with her. But for now I was proud of the story.

I sent a copy to Antwon: *Thought you might want to see this. Would love your feedback.*

Several days later, Antwon called. "Sure," he said, "let's talk about it. How about meeting at my office?" He gave me an address. It was only when I arrived that I realized it was for an Italian pastry shop in the East Village. I stopped at the counter and bought a plate of cookies and a cappuccino before proceeding to the back, where Antwon was sitting at a corner table.

"Nice office," I said. "It's better than mine. I work in publishing—did Don tell you? My desk is shoved into a tiny cubicle. But my boss calls it an 'office,' not a 'cube,' because she wants me to feel important. She has a real office, with a framed Hannah Hoch poster above her desk. When she wants something from me, she knocks on the flimsy partitioning and asks, 'Can I come in your office?' It all feels so silly."

"Come in my office," Antwon said, and pulled out a chair.

I had come straight from work, and I felt self-conscious about my outfit—khakis and an oxford shirt with a button-down collar—which must have seemed preppy to Antwon. He was wearing a black T-shirt and jeans and heavy, black-rimmed glasses I didn't recognize from the two or three times I had met him out at bars. On the table in front of him was an espresso, a copy of my story (pristine: no dog-eared pages, no marks, at least none that I could see), and a legal pad flipped open to an empty page, a fancy pen resting diagonally across it.

I asked him if he had read the story. He grunted yes. I expected him to elaborate, but he didn't. I was still new to writing and insecure about my work. I wanted to ask him if he liked the story, but I didn't want to sound needy. I didn't want to admit to Antwon there was anything I needed from him. I finally asked, "Any suggestions?"

Antwon thought for several seconds then said, "Not really. I'm not the best person to ask. I'm not good at giving feedback."

We nibbled at the cookies. They were so pretty, I had bought them forgetting I didn't like that kind. I asked Antwon questions about the reading series, the venue, the other readers. We didn't talk about my story.

Just before it was time for me to leave, I again tried to muster courage to ask if he liked my story. But I asked instead, "What do you think of the sex scenes?" I thought: *This you can comment on. Isn't it your specialty?*

He asked, "Which specifically? The description of the photos in the porn mag or the masturbation scene in the car?"

"Either. Both."

He scanned a few pages, thought for a moment. "Is the word 'rare' really necessary?" It took me a minute to realize he was referring to my description of drops of Rocco's come on Lacey's breasts as "rare pearls." He said, "Aren't pearls 'rare' by definition?"

"I'm not sure I'm looking for line edits here. I'm wondering more about the thrust of it." I blushed at the pun.

Antwon removed his glasses, lifted his gaze to the ceiling, clasped his hands behind his head. "I was interested in how boring the sex scenes were." He chuckled and said, "That's nothing against your piece. Honestly. I think it's true of all sex scenes. They're always boring. What words do we have to describe sex? The terms are either clinical and sterile or they are childish and comical. It's impossible to get sex right."

"What about your own sex scenes?" I asked. "Are they boring?"

"That's not for me to say. It's for others to judge." After a moment, he said, "You, for instance. Do *you* find my sex scenes boring?"

"I've never read your work."

I couldn't tell if he knew I was lying.

I pushed the plate of cookies toward him. "I don't like these," I said. "I don't like anise."

As I was leaving, I turned around and saw Antwon biting into one.

The reading, when it rolled around, was fine. I was nervous. As the least-published of the four writers (*un*published, in fact), I read first. When Antwon introduced me, he said nothing about my work, my bio, my qualifications, only, "I met this writer through my friend Don."

Afterward, my cousin came up to congratulate me. He was an investment banker and showed up in a suit. He smiled mischievously and said, "I know how those West Virginia back roads are," referring to the geography both my narrator and myself shared. I wanted to tell him just because he recognized some of the details didn't mean the story was true. I wanted to take him through line by line, noting every exaggeration, every misrepresentation, every fantasy and lie. Instead, I said, simply, "I did *not* jack off in my parents' Dodge Caravan," although, in truth, I had. I told him my friends were taking me out for a drink and asked if he wanted to join. He said no, he had to return to the office. I pointed out it was almost midnight. He said something about Asian markets and left.

Several of my friends were in the audience, too, and they waited their turn to talk to me. It was my first time reading one of my stories, and I was grateful for their goodwill. But I wasn't listening to what they were saying. Instead, I was looking around, searching for Antwon.

I spotted him across the room talking to the guy who wrote for the *Village Voice* and who had read an essay about growing up in Rochester and the woman next door who had taught him how to be a drag queen. Everyone seemed to want to talk to Antwon. It made sense. The reading was as much about him, the curator, as it was about us, the readers. Besides, he was more established and better known than any of us. Don pointed out, swirling around Antwon, several luminaries from the downtown scene: an F-to-M transsexual sex columnist; a performance artist who referred to herself as "A Woman Who Just So Happens to Have a Beard"; a cabaret artist whose cult following included Parker Posey, Debbie Harry, and Courtney Love (when she was in town). I waited a long time to talk to Antwon, hovering close to him, searching for an opening, but I never found one. I finally left.

In the coming weeks, I waited to hear from him. I waited for him to invite me to his office. I would dress better this time and order a cannoli instead of those cookies. He would smile at me from across the table and say, "I'm glad I asked you to read. Everyone was impressed. *I* was impressed." But he didn't call.

The next time Don came home from meeting Antwon (Dick's: draft), he didn't say if Antwon mentioned the reading or if he mentioned me, and I didn't allow myself to ask.

3.

When I arrived at Don's house, climbed the back stairs, opened the door with my extra key, the first person I saw was Antwon, standing at the stove stirring soup. He was shirtless, the hair on his chest shot through with gray. He and Don must have just come from the studio. They were sweaty and seemed hungry. Antwon was cooking from the vegetarian cookbook he gave Don and me as a housewarming gift five years ago when we first moved in together in Crown Heights. It lay next to the stove, open to the recipe for mulligatawny soup, a dish I had been eating my whole life and didn't need a recipe to make.

"Taste," he said, and scooped up a spoonful. He blew on it, cupped a hand beneath, and held it out to Don, who was also shirtless, sitting at a small table.

I watched as Don let himself be fed.

The previous fall, Don and I had moved to upstate New York, just a few hours from New York City, but a world away. It was my idea; I wanted to go to grad school for creative writing. I told Don I couldn't do it in the city; it was too distracting. He was reluctant to move, but he eventually conceded. He found a graduate program in dance. Our schools were two hours apart, and we took turns visiting each other on weekends.

Don was renting the upstairs apartment in a small house a block from campus. His landlord was a farmer who lived in the next town over. When he showed us the apartment, he was wearing jeans and work boots caked in mud. He didn't remove them before walking all over the carpet. He also didn't say anything about the downstairs neighbors.

Several days after Don had moved into his apartment and I had moved into mine, Don told me he still hadn't met them or even seen them. But he'd *heard* them. He said during the day, their blinds were closed, their windows and doors shut. But several nights a week, around two or three in the morning, Don woke to the *thump thump thump* of their stereo blasting techno music. He said he could feel it pulsating through the thin floor. After a few weeks, one night when I was sleeping over and hearing the din for myself, Don said, "Enough," threw back the covers, splashed water on his face, and padded downstairs to talk to them. When he returned, the volume was maybe microscopically lower, maybe not. "What happened?" I asked. He said, "I don't know what those boys are on—coke, speed, crystal meth. Their eyes were like Frisbees. I'm not going back down there."

It had been a difficult year. We weren't prepared for the cold, gray winter that seemed like it would never end. It was particularly difficult for Don, because he didn't like his program, which was reputable but stale. The best-known faculty member choreographed Broadway musicals. Don's work, by contrast, was experimental. In so many ways, he felt like an alien.

That was why he had invited Antwon, why he had spent so much time convincing the other members of the visiting guest artist committee that Antwon would be perfect for a one-week residency. Don was frustrated and craved the creative boost that would accompany Antwon's visit. He also hoped that, as a byproduct of meeting Antwon, the students and faculty would have a greater understanding and appreciation for Don's own edgy work.

When he first told me he was thinking about bringing Antwon, I thought about saying no. Antwon had been out of our lives, more or less, for almost a year, and I was grateful. But I held my tongue, thinking, *Don needs this*. And now here he was, feeding Don soup. He'd been here all week teaching classes; these were the last two days.

To cap off the residency, Antwon was planning to perform one of his own pieces at an informal student concert that night and the next. I'd never seen his work and wasn't quite sure what to expect, though I knew, of course, Don loved it.

Antwon's piece was titled *Yours*. He described it as an exercise in "relinquishing control" and "surrendering to the desires of others." The performance worked like this. Antwon would pick three people from the audience and ask them to stand on the side of the stage. They would each be responsible for a body part, controlling whether he saw, spoke or moved by saying *eyes*, *mouth*, or *body*. Then Antwon would pick someone else to stand at the other edge of the stage with six large cards numbered five through zero in descending order. The audience would determine the length of the performance because whenever anyone got bored that person could call out the number on the card—*five!*—which the person holding the cards would then drop, revealing the next number in descending order. The numbers would get called one by one until the audience reached zero and the dance was over. Anyone from the audience could call out a number whenever he or she got bored. It was perfectly democratic.

The first night, the performance didn't last long. The audience wasn't interested in Antwon. Most of the other dances featured pretty girls and MTV choreography or classical ballet, and when the girls performed, their parents and boyfriends cheered and whistled and snapped photos. When Antwon performed, they read their programs and looked at their watches, wondering if they'd get home in time to watch their favorite television shows. They called out numbers five to zero quick as a space-shuttle countdown.

At home that night, Antwon was demoralized. "That was one of the worst concerts and worst audiences I've ever encountered, and I've been performing a long time."

"Actually, I kind of liked the routine to Britney's 'Stronger,'" I said, "especially the part where the girl jumped off the ballet barre." I was partly joking, partly not—a tone Don was familiar with by now.

Don and Antwon were sitting close to each other on the couch. Don leaned over to him and said, "See what I've been dealing with." I assumed he was responding to what Antwon had said about the crappy concert and the unappreciative audience, not to my comment about liking the Britney routine, though I couldn't be sure. They continued grumbling among themselves and popping caps off beer after beer, and after a while I got tired. I disappeared into the bedroom without anyone noticing or saying goodnight.

The next morning Antwon said he wanted to see Niagara Falls. We were only a couple of hours away. "This is probably the closest I'll ever get, so I might as well." Neither Don nor I had seen the Falls either.

"I don't have my passport," I said. Don and Antwon both had theirs: Don because we were in his apartment and Antwon because he didn't have a driver's license, so it was his main form of ID. My passport was in my own apartment, two hours away.

Don said, "American citizens don't need passports to cross into Canada."

"True," I said, "if you're *white*." I looked at Antwon, expecting him to back me up, but he didn't say anything.

Don said, "Stop playing the race card."

I told them the story of my one failed attempt to see the Falls.

"My cousin's grandmother was visiting from India, and we agreed to take her. My cousin and I were both eighteen or so. We drove in my uncle's car all the way from Poughkeepsie, seven hours away, and when we reached the border we were denied entry. Well, my cousin and I were denied entry. My cousin's grandmother was fine; she had her passport, a visa, everything. But we only had driver's licenses. 'Anyone can get a driver's license,' the guard insisted. My cousin said, 'Our car has New York plates.' I said, 'We're driving a Mercedes.' But the guard was unmoved. So we found a tour bus in Buffalo that would take my cousin's grandmother across the border, and my cousin and I waited for three hours in a Friendly's parking lot, smoking cigarettes. But it was worth it. She loved it, and talked about it the whole way home. My cousin said she was still talking about it when she called him from India two months later."

"You could have seen the Falls from the American side," Don said. "You didn't have to sit in a parking lot."

"The American side isn't as good. You only get one first time, and a girl wants hers to be special." I made doe eyes at him and batted my eyelashes, which he didn't seem to notice, but Antwon winked at me.

"I don't want to ruin it for everyone," I said. "You guys should go on your own."

Don and Antwon exchanged glances. I imagined them hopping into the car—*my* car, probably, since it was the more reliable of the two—and peeling out of the driveway, all too happy to be sailing away without me. Sailors at sea, where anything could happen. I'd be alone in Don's apartment, scrubbing the breakfast dishes. I suddenly felt sick.

"Don't be silly," Don said. "You're coming."

"What if they don't let me in? I'm not spending another three hours in the parking lot of Friendly's."

"They will," Don said. "If they don't, we'll come back. It's a nice day for a drive."

It was true. It was a beautiful spring day, the first after a long, difficult winter.

When we arrived at the border, the guard asked our citizenship. He asked where we were going. He asked if we were carrying fruits or vegetables or firearms. He asked to see what was in our trunk (jumper cables; tools; a bag of old clothes for the Salvation Army, which had been there since we packed up our Crown Heights apartment the previous August). Then he waved us through.

"Toldja," Don said from the driver's seat. He pecked me on the cheek, and I found myself half-wishing we had been turned away, just to have been right.

A few minutes later and we were at the Falls. As we walked toward them, I was unimpressed. "I thought they'd be bigger." I was distracted by the hordes of tourists: fat Americans; endless busloads of Chinese; Indian aunties—not unlike my own cousin's grandmother—in saris and cardigans and chappals and thick wool socks. It was nothing like I had imagined.

Don and Antwon, on the other hand, were mesmerized. The three of us walked up close, eventually leaning over the railing of the platform that hovered above the Falls. Antwon tried to say something to me, but I couldn't hear him over the sound of the water. And for a moment it was nice to stand there, sandwiched between Don and Antwon, the mist on my face, the crashing water so loud it drowned out everything else. Nothing else existed. The world fell away. I had the most pleasant sensation of being both there and not there. I wondered if that was how the boys downstairs felt when they blasted their music.

Later, in the pavilion, as we were eating our veggie burgers, I asked Antwon what he was trying to tell me at the Falls.

"Forget it," he said.

"No," Don said, in a mock-jealous voice, "what were you two whispering about?"

"As if anyone could have been whispering and still be heard," I said.

Antwon said, "I was just thinking: people must die here all the time. Personally, I always have the urge to jump. Not that I want to die. My mind never even gets that far. It's not about dying. It's about wanting to know what it feels like to float, or fly, or fall, or whatever it feels like. It's about wanting to feel free. Haven't you guys ever had that urge?"

Don said, "Yes, always. Leaning over the Falls, the edge of a cliff, the railing at the Empire State Building."

"What about you?" Antwon asked me.

"I'm not sure," I said. "I guess I have."

"If you're not sure, then you haven't," Antwon said.

I tried to picture it—climbing over the railing, leaping outward. Maybe I'd do it farther upstream, diving into the river, letting myself get swept away toward the Falls. Would I try to grab onto something at the last minute? Or would I let it happen?

Later, driving home, Don said, "Someone from our school recently died here."

"Someone I knew?" I asked.

"No. He was a video artist. Not much older than I am. Last summer, his baby had a high fever, and he and his wife took her to the emergency room. After a couple of hours, the hospital staff started asking them questions that had nothing to do with the fever. The hospital told them they would have to leave their baby, she was being held overnight until the fever subsided, and then she would be released into the custody of Child Welfare.

"According to the rumor mill, the authorities thought the couple was abusing the child, but no one seems to know what made the authorities think that or specifically what they think the couple did. The couple spent the next several months racking up legal bills they couldn't pay, trying to get their baby back. Then one day, the husband got in his car, drove to the Falls, and threw himself in. No warning. No note. At his funeral, the wife showed some of his recent video work, which he had been shooting for months, and which consisted mostly of slow-motion, black-and-white videos of the Falls, mostly in winter. Everyone cried, even the people who barely knew him."

We continued driving. I was in the passenger seat and had taken control of the radio. When the new Janet Jackson song came on, I danced in my seat. From the highway, I could see the tacky yellow sign of a regional discount chain, and I asked Don if we could stop. I wanted to buy the CD. Antwon said he had to pee.

As we veered onto the exit ramp, Antwon asked, "Do you think he planned it? Do you think he drove the two hours knowing what he would ultimately do? Or do you think he was just planning to shoot video as usual and, leaning over the Falls, found himself unable to resist?"

"Do you think it was guilt?" I asked. "Do you think he'd actually done something to the baby?" No one said anything. I wondered if they thought I was mean for asking.

The discount chain was in a depressing town just off the interstate. The customers were mostly families, mostly rural poor: the men in work boots, like Don's landlord; the younger women with peroxide hair, the older ones in elastic waistbands. I felt vaguely worried Antwon would get jumped in the restroom. There was no reason for my concern: these people were as nice as the next. But Antwon rarely left the city, he didn't understand rural America. So I was relieved when he met up with me at the checkout. At the last minute, I grabbed a Dolly Parton greatest-hits compilation from the discount bin by the register.

In the car, Don said, "Driver's choice," and insisted we hear Dolly first, since we'd already heard the Janet Jackson song three times on the radio.

The first track was "Jolene."

"This song was inspired by a hot bank teller," I told them. "I read it in an interview. It was early in her marriage, and Dolly was jealous when she noticed her husband was making more and more trips to the bank."

The next song was "Coat of Many Colors." We listened to it, and a couple more tracks, and then we reached "I Will Always Love You."

"I didn't know Dolly recorded this, too," I said.

"Too?" Antwon said. "It's *her* song. This is the original."

"Really? I thought the original was Whitney Houston."

We listened to Dolly's country twang, so different from the way Whitney's voice climbed and soared. By the time the song's bridge came around, Dolly wasn't even singing, she was simply talking; her voice had dropped to a whisper.

Antwon said, "This version makes so much more sense. It's less about the 'I' and more about the 'you.'"

Something about Antwon's comment made me mad. I thought, *Who is he to judge?* Besides, I liked Whitney's cover. "Whitney's version has sold more than Dolly's," I said. "It's one of the best-selling singles of all time."

"There's little connection between popularity and quality, believe me. Besides, Whitney's version is all flash. It doesn't have any of the honesty or regret of Dolly's. Saying good-bye to someone you love doesn't sound like a gospel choir. There aren't so many runs. It feels plainer, more like Dolly's version, more like a whisper."

Don said he agreed with Antwon. I thought about Antwon saying good-bye to Don when we left New York. What did they say to one another? Where had they eaten their last dinner? I'd never asked.

Don hadn't given me permission to switch the CD yet, but I did it anyway, popping in the Janet Jackson, skipping right away to the single that was getting so much airplay. This time I not only danced in my seat, I sang along: "Got nice package alright / Guess I'm gonna have to ride it tonight."

"Are those really the lyrics?" Antwon asked.

Janet's Super Bowl "wardrobe malfunction" was three years away. For now—despite the sexy videos and the *Rolling Stone* cover with the hands over her bare breasts—she was still America's sweetheart, the adorable baby girl of the Jackson clan, everyone's little sister, her cheeks eminently and forever pinchable.

"It's amazing what Janet gets away with," I said.

"It doesn't seem fair," Antwon said.

When we got home, Antwon asked to see the store receipt from the CDs, and he dialed the phone number on the slip.

"I'd like to speak with the manager." After waiting, he continued, "Yes, sir, I am calling to make a complaint. I have been shopping at your store for years. I was in there not one hour ago. I was there with my family: my wife and my son. I wanted duct tape. My wife wanted socks. Anyway, my son comes to me with a CD he found in the music department, and I say, *Sure, you can have it*, thinking to myself, This is a family establishment, a clean, Christian establishment. No reason not to buy my son a CD he found on the shelves. Well, when we got home, I went to duct taping the ... errr ... duct, and my wife is fixing dinner in the kitchen, and my son plays the CD on the kitchen stereo—son? What's the name of that CD? Yes! Janet Jackson—and, sir, can I just read you some of these lyrics?" Antwon proceeded to read the lyrics, carefully and dramatically enunciating every syllable: "'Got nice package alright / Guess I'm gonna have to ride it tonight.' Now, sir, I'm guessing you and I both know she's not singing about a UPS delivery, right? We know what she means. And, worse, my *son* knows what she means. Yes, sir, I understand. Yes, sir. Well, we appreciate that. And now that you know what's contained in this CD, I trust you won't stock such ... such ... *trash*, there's no other way to say it ... any longer."

Antwon hung up. "We can return the CD for cash plus five-dollar store credit."

Don and I burst out laughing, we had been holding it in the whole time. Antwon should have been laughing, too, but he wasn't. At some point during the phone call, his tone had shifted, and he seemed genuinely mad, but I couldn't figure out why.

Antwon disappeared into the bathroom to start getting ready for his performance that night.

I thought about what he had said in the car about it not being fair.

I remembered an art book he had given Don, and which I had found on the same bookshelf where I'd discovered the anthology of gay erotica. It was a book of photographs by Robert Mapplethorpe, whose name came up often when Congress made its fuss over public funding of art. I was thinking now of a particular self-portrait: Mapplethorpe in bottomless leather chaps, his naked, hairy asshole wrapped around the thick handle of a bullwhip. In the photo, he is turned around, looking over his shoulder at the camera, fully meeting the gaze of the viewer. He is offering a challenge. He is trying to shock us. Yet there is a softness to his expression. He looks, more than anything, vulnerable. The photo was included among those that the Corcoran Gallery in D.C. refused to display, even though the gallery had promised Mapplethorpe it would. The artist had died of AIDS just three or four months before the gallery reneged on its word. If Mapplethorpe were alive now, I thought, he'd be just a few years older than Antwon.

I could hear Antwon cursing in the bathroom. "Don, do you have any aftershave?" he shouted, and Don said no.

"What does aftershave do?" I asked. I'd never used it, though I seemed to remember that my dad did.

"It's an antiseptic," Don explained.

A minute later Antwon was still cursing, and I went in to see what was wrong. He had cut himself. He was standing at the mirror, blood on his chin. He was in his underwear: white cotton briefs. They made him look young.

"Let me put a Band-Aid," I said. He was taller than I was, and when I put the Band-Aid on I had to lean in close and I lost my balance. My forearms touched his chest. It was warm and clean from his shower.

His cheeks smelled like mouthwash.

"Did you put Listerine on your face?" I asked.

"It's the same as aftershave."

"No, it's not."

"Yes, it is." He looked at me and smiled, and for a second I thought he was going to pinch my cheek, but instead he slapped my ass and called me a pet name I'd never been called before: *Squirrel.* I thought of the enchanted creatures in the forest who stood in for Prince Charming before Sleeping Beauty found her real one. I thought of Rocky and Bullwinkle, a bickering gay couple if I'd ever seen one. I thought of hoarding: how—after moving upstate—whenever I visited New York City, I would imagine each art exhibit, each dance concert, each drag show, each cultural excursion as an acorn, and if I collected enough I might just make it through the long winter. I remembered myself, a few years ago, not long after I started dating Don, on a couch in the back of a bar (a different couch and a different bar from where Don first told me about Antwon, though they are all the same), sitting in the lap of an older man, contemplating cheating on Don, fingering the older man's gold ring: Married? *Was.* Was? *He died.* How? (Pause.) *The usual way.* (Even longer pause—his body tense, then relaxed—then in a jarring, cheerful voice ...) *But I'm a healthy squirrel.*

I didn't go home with the man that night. Now, I smoothed the Band-Aid over Antwon's chin, allowing my finger to drift down his neck, across his chest, circling the gray hairs. Antwon remained frozen. He looked confused. The door was open. Don was in the kitchen, just down the hall. I didn't know why I was doing it, but it felt good. Antwon's body felt good. I ran my fingers down his torso—his dancer's abs still taut but beginning to soften with age—and over his cotton briefs, tracing the contours of his hip.

A ntwon said he'd figured out a way to solve the problems from the previous night's performance. Instead of "surrendering to the desire of others," he was only going to surrender to the desires of a few preselected people whom he himself had screened and approved. He would choose five of us—me and Don and three of his pet students from his class that week. Four of us would be in charge of calling out the numbers, and one student would hold the numbered cards. *We* would determine the length of the dance instead of the audience. Then he would preselect three more pet students—one to say *eyes*, one to say *mouth*, one to say *body*—so there would be eight of us total, standing on the side of the stage, controlling him.

The dance began. *Mouth*.

"This past week I haven't been able to sleep. The downstairs neighbors are loud, but I don't think that's it."

The girl said *mouth* again, and Antwon stopped talking.

Eyes. Antwon, blinded, ambled to the front row of the audience, almost tripping over a man sitting in a chair. It was an elderly man, perhaps the grandfather of one of the students performing. Antwon stroked his legs. Then he sat in his lap and caressed his face. In another venue, in New York for instance, people would have been laughing. Here they were not. Antwon stood up and started moving toward the back of the stage.

Body. He froze. *Eyes*. He opened them wide, stood silent and still, fully meeting the gaze of the viewers.

Mouth. "I couldn't sleep in New York either. It's been over a year since I slept soundly."

Mouth. *Body*. *Eyes*. All in quick succession. Antwon stumbled around. He looked lost. He settled into some simple gestures, mostly elbows and hands.

Mouth, the girl said again. "That's when my mom died: a year ago. We were very close, though I hadn't seen her in a long time. She lived in Indiana, where I was born and raised. Thirty years I lived in New York, and she never visited, not once. Never saw me perform. When she died, she left me a Cutlass Supreme. I don't know how to drive. I've never known how to drive."

Body. Antwon was standing still again, staring into the audience. "She also left me her life's savings—seventeen thousand dollars—which I added to some money I'd saved over the years. I used it all for a down payment on an apartment in Chinatown off Grand Street. Now I live down the street from my ex-wife, whom I married before I became a full-time fudge-packer and she became a full-time donut-banger, though we should have known, even then, that that was the way it was going to go. Not that I regret it. What's to regret? Fudge and donuts? It's not such a bad combination. Back then, she aborted our child. Now I babysit the daughter she adopted with her partner."

A middle-aged man and woman stood up angrily and angled their way toward the exit. Others followed.

"Mouth!" a rogue audience member shouted, *not* the girl on the side of the stage who had been designated to say *mouth*. Then she said *mouth*, too, echoing the audience member. But Antwon didn't stop speaking. Maybe he was confused. Or maybe he was deliberately ignoring the orders he'd been given.

"My mother was my only family, the only family I know of. Now I am alone."

Mouth, the designated student said more emphatically this time, and Antwon stopped.

Body. Antwon hustled toward the back of the stage, then threw himself against the back wall, repeatedly, violently, as though he were trying to put back in place a dislocated shoulder.

He fell to the floor and thrashed around. I wondered if he hurt himself.

He was still wearing the Band-Aid I had smoothed on his chin.

We'd closed his eyes. We'd shut his mouth.

The audience was bored or, worse, hostile. They were beginning to snicker at him.

They didn't understand.

We'd been counting down numbers all along, and I looked over at the student holding the cards and noticed we were down to one. I called it out and then less than a minute later, *zero*. I watched the card fall to the floor and slide a little toward Antwon.

The bass from the neighbors' stereo reached up through the floor and shook me awake. I squinted at the clock: four a.m. I got out of bed and stumbled toward the bathroom. I could hear the shower from the hallway. When I entered the bathroom, I could see it was on full blast. Antwon was next to it, lying flat on the bathroom floor. He had dragged his pillows and blanket with him.

"How can you live like this?" He had to shout to be heard over the noise.

The shower helped muffle the techno, but only a little.

I said, "I have to pee."

"Who's stopping you?"

I stepped over him, lifted the toilet seat, hooked my thumb in the waistband of my pajamas, tugged them down. I hadn't switched on the bathroom light; the only light was from the hallway. As I was pissing, I looked to see if Antwon was watching, but I couldn't tell in the shadows. I briefly imagined myself swiveling my hips. I pictured the stream of piss hitting his face, his chest. Would he have been insulted? Or turned on? Which would I have preferred?

On my way out, as I was stepping over him, I stopped for a moment, lingering. My legs straddled his body. My knees bent ever so slightly. I started to lower myself onto him. Then I stopped, straightened, took a step to leave. As I did this, did I feel his hand briefly grasp the cuff of my pajama? Did I hear— through the thump of the techno, through the crash of the shower—a murmur, a whisper? *Squirrel. Stay.*

The next morning was another beautiful day, so we decided to leave for the airport early and to stop at a park for a picnic. Antwon had a new laptop computer, and he was afraid to put it in the trunk because he said it would get too hot, and he was afraid to leave it in the backseat because he said someone would steal it, so we took turns carrying it as we hiked through the woods to the picnic spot. When it was my turn, I complained loudly about how heavy it was, though it was fairly light, which everyone, of course, knew.

After we found our spot and settled down, Antwon asked if we wanted to see a funny photo of him. He pulled out an expired passport stowed in the front compartment of his laptop case, where he also stored his current passport. The passport must have been almost thirty years old. Antwon's name was listed as "Clarence." He said he'd changed it when he moved to New York.

"Why do you keep this?" Don asked.

"I don't know," he said.

I didn't recognize Antwon in the photo. He looked stoned. Defiant. His neck was thick, his jaw squared, his head tilted backward. He was gap-toothed, his hair in an enormous Afro.

He is sexy, I thought, looking at the photo. I thought it again later that night in bed with Don, and two nights later in bed alone in my own apartment, and many nights after that.

Don napped in the sun, and Antwon told me stories about dodging the draft, fucking his way across Europe and the Middle East, living in a kibbutz in Israel, which apparently was a popular thing to do at the time, even if you weren't Jewish. I'd never done any of those things or been to any of those places.

"My dad dodged the draft, too," I said. "But he was only successful for so long. It finally came down to a lottery, and if he got picked he probably would have gone back to India instead of serving, and I'd be living there now instead of here."

Antwon told me his ex-wife was Martina—a friend of Don's, a performance artist who sometimes went by "Martin" and whom I had met many times, but I never knew she'd been married to Antwon. He said she didn't tell him about the abortion until much later, until it was over. He said, "Not that it would have changed anything."

He told me when he first moved to New York he shared a studio apartment with a cast member of the original production of *A Chorus Line*, when it was still off-Broadway, long before anyone knew or even dreamed what it would become. He said he'd been asked to do some of the choreography, but had said no. He said if he had said yes, maybe he'd be rich now. Or maybe the show would have flopped. Who knew?

I was impressed by the life Antwon had led, the life he continued to lead. Impressed in the same way I'd been at the reading he curated, watching as the downtown luminaries swirled around him. Impressed in the same way Don must have been when he first took a class with Antwon, so many years ago, when he first saw Antwon perform. I tried to think of stories to tell

Antwon, stories about my own life that might impress him, but nothing compared.

When it was time for us to leave, Don insisted there was a shortcut back to the car, and he led us down a different path that turned into a field that became a swamp.

"These are my new sneakers," I whined, as the mud gulped at my shoes. "This is the worst thing that has ever happened to me."

Antwon laughed. "I sincerely hope this *is* the worst thing that's ever happened to you, and that ever will."

4.

The following fall, in a memoir-writing class in grad school, I tried to write about it: about me and Don and Antwon. When I met with my professor, a famous memoirist, to discuss my draft, I noticed she referred to all my characters as just that, as *characters*, not as real people, even though I was presumably writing about myself and people in my life. She would say to me "the narrator," not "you," as though this character just happened to have the same name as I did.

She said, "When your narrator says, *There are things only a lover knows*, he should give examples."

She said, "The piece seems to be tiptoeing around race. It's not clear enough to the reader that Antwon is black."

"Race is incidental," I said.

"You're wrong," she said. "It's a big part of what your piece is about."

"It's about desire," I said.

She said, "It's about control."

She said, "Your readers will want to know why the narrator never confronts Don about whether or not he had sex with Antwon in exchange for money, why he never demands to know definitively. It seems ridiculous that your narrator doesn't ask. Your narrator owes it to your readers to explain his rationale. If he doesn't, your readers will think he's holding back."

She said, "They won't like him. They won't like *you*."

After leaving her office, I walked to a nearby café, which was closing in another month because a Starbucks had opened down the street. No one was sad about this; the coffee was terrible. But I was happy to be there. It had big couches and, since everyone had already switched to Starbucks, it was empty. I wanted to be alone.

I wondered about the memoirist's question. Why hadn't I cornered Don? Why hadn't I insisted he tell me everything?

Around the time Don and I first moved in together and I discovered Antwon's story, Mayor Giuliani had mounted an effort to "clean up the city," as he called it. He started using antiquated zoning laws, which hadn't been enforced in decades, to shut down strip bars and sex clubs. To many of us, it seemed like he was particularly targeting establishments with a queer clientele.

Two of our closest friends, Priscilla and Charlene—lovers and PhD students at Columbia—joined a group called SexPanic! They did things like stand outside the mayor's office, holding signs, chanting, "We're here! We're queer! We fuck strangers on the pier! Get used to it!" Priscilla occasionally worked as a stripper at the Blue Angel. She said we wouldn't believe the types she met there. She once got paid four hundred bucks for shitting on a plate in a room in the St. Marks Hotel, while her client masturbated. Her dissertation was somehow connected to all this, but I wasn't sure how.

In a few years, Priscilla and Charlene would move to Wisconsin, leaving behind SexPanic! and the Blue Angel. They would settle into more or less quiet academic lives. But at the time, their lives seemed to me messy with passion. I admired them, in a way, and wanted to believe what they believed, though I couldn't quite articulate what that was. Something about living fully and dangerously. Something about sexual freedom. It seemed to me to be the same thing that Antwon, years later, would describe at the Falls, when he talked about the urge to jump, about wanting to feel that feeling of floating or flying or falling, about wanting to feel free.

If I had asked Don directly what had happened between him and Antwon, he would have told me, I have no doubt. But I didn't want to ask. Not that I didn't want to know. I *did* want to know. But I didn't want to want to know. I didn't want to *need* to know.

The memoir-writing class had forced me to see this more clearly. It had also gotten me to think about something else: about the process of how writers transform the experiences of their lives. I remembered my own reading of my story, "The Night Jagdish Learned to Drive," my cousin's comment afterward, the lie I'd told him.

The next weekend, when I visited Don, I dug out the anthology of gay erotica with Antwon's story, no longer on my bookshelf, but now in Don's closet in a cardboard box with a broken VCR and an old thesaurus. I hadn't read Antwon's story in years. Even now, it was difficult. I remembered the first time, lying on the floor in the one-bedroom in Crown Heights, I had to keep stopping, putting the book down. The boy in the story winces as he is fucked for the first time ever. That is the word the narrator uses: "winces." The boy is described "baring his teeth," and afterward, "crying quietly."

Reading the story again now, I told myself: Don wasn't trying to be coy or deceptive when he said it wasn't him. It *wasn't* him. It *isn't* him. It isn't any of us.

Even when it is.

5.

A few months later, I ran into Antwon, almost literally, on Second Avenue in the East Village. He smelled like cologne. He was holding a red rose.

"Thank you," I said, and reached for it.

"It's for me," he said. He didn't say who gave it to him. "Today I'm half a century old."

"Wow. Are you celebrating?"

"I'm on my way to meet some friends at John's."

"That's Don's favorite restaurant."

"Mine, too," he said.

"A coincidence," I said, understanding that perhaps it wasn't.

Antwon rolled the stem of the rose between his fingers, and then held the blossom to his nose, breathing in deeply, half-shutting his eyes. He seemed to be considering something for a moment. He started to speak, then stopped.

After a few seconds, he said, "What are you doing here?"

"In New York? It was an impromptu trip. The day before, we had gone to the grocery store and we'd noticed that tomatoes were on sale. There was a sign above the display that read: *In Celebration of Black History Month—Tomatoes are a key ingredient in African-American cooking.* There was something so sad about that sign. I thought, *This is the way we celebrate black history? Tomatoes on sale?* We had to get out of there."

"You have good timing," Antwon said. He pulled a card from his coat pocket and handed it to me. I looked at it. On the front was an image of Antwon in a Mohawk (which he wasn't sporting now) and blindfolded by a pair of black lace stockings. On the back were details for his show at The Kitchen. The only time I'd seen Antwon perform were those nights when he visited us upstate. "Tomorrow and Sunday are the last two days," he said. "Please come."

"I will," I said.

Later, while walking to the movie theater where I was meeting Don and some of our friends, I caught myself absentmindedly chewing on the corner of his postcard, a nervous habit from when I was a kid.

Two days later, Don and I and our friend, with whom we were staying, were eating bagels in the kitchen. It was a bright morning, and the sun streamed into the room through a dirty window that opened out onto a fire escape. We were all quietly reading our separate sections of the *Times* when Don said excitedly, "Look," and pointed out a review of Antwon's performance. He read it out loud. It was glowing, an unequivocal rave. "Unsentimental," Don read. "Achingly honest. The choreographer masterfully leads the performers, and by extension the audience, into complicated emotional terrain. The result is both terrifying and seductive."

We had all planned to attend that night. "It's a good thing we already have reservations," our friend said. "It's sure to be sold out now."

I got up to fetch some orange juice and noticed, stuck to the refrigerator door with a magnet, the postcard of Antwon with the Mohawk, the one he gave me when I ran into him on the street. My bite marks perforated the corner.

When I sat back down, Don was still looking at the paper, rereading the article. His eyes were wide, his mouth smiling broadly.

That evening, I was sitting in the living room when Don came into the room and said it was time to go to the performance. I was wearing track pants and a sloppy T-shirt, and I was splayed out on the couch, clutching the remote control, my eyes fixed on the TV.

"I'm not going."

"Why?" Don asked.

I looked away from the screen. Don was standing there in a tailored dress shirt and designer jeans he had bought at Century 21 during an earlier trip. His brow was furrowed. He was holding his wool peacoat in his hands.

There were so many things I could have said.

"I'm feeling sick."

Don looked at me a moment. I could tell he was considering calling my bluff, forcing me to explain why I didn't want to go. But then he seemed to decide against it. He kissed me on the forehead, gently, as though I were really sick. "Feel better."

After Don and our friend left, I considered leaving, too. I could have walked down the block, seen a movie, eaten sushi, bought a chocolate croissant at my favorite patisserie. After all, it was one of my precious few nights in the city—a night to collect acorns. Instead, I got sucked into the television, idly flipping through channels, eventually settling on a marathon of reruns of *Friends*, a show I'd hated when it first started airing back when I still lived here, hated in part for being such a patently false version of a life in New York. But now that it was in syndication, now that I no longer lived here, I found it comforting, even sweet. I fell asleep before Don returned.

In the car the next day, barely out of New York, barreling down the highway past the bland New Jersey suburbs—an endless parade of Targets and Borders and Bon-Tons—I asked Don about the performance. I was driving. Don took a moment. He lowered the volume on the radio, turned his whole body toward me, lifted his hands (Don, ever the dancer, talked with his whole body). He took a deep breath. The way he did this, I could tell he was ready to launch into an animated description of some section he loved, some particular bit of movement that reminded him of why he himself had become a dancer in the first place. But then he exhaled and said, "You know, it wasn't so great." I glanced at him. "Really?" He smiled. "I'm sorry to say it: Antwon is over-rated." Don faced front, turned up the radio, and sank back into his seat.

That morning we'd heard on the weather forecast about a blizzard that was expected to develop that evening. The report warned it was going to paralyze the whole region. The first few flakes were just beginning to fall. They hit the windshield—heavy and wet—and the wipers wiped them away. I gripped the wheel and, hoping to beat the worst of it, gently pressed my foot on the accelerator.

NINE   *A Better Life*

When, by the end of the summer of 1990, the summer they graduated from high school, Sylvie had not only *not* lost the ten pounds the modeling agency had wanted her to lose, but she had, instead, *gained* fifteen pounds, she was told she shouldn't bother coming to New York, the agency couldn't represent her, they couldn't find her work. She was told this over the phone by a woman she had met in New York in the spring, an "ugly" woman, Sylvie now said, whom no one could ever find pretty, so who was she to judge?

Sanj saw Sylvie that Sunday night, two nights after she'd received the news, and just three days before he himself was leaving for the University of Southern California—as far from West

Virginia as he could manage. Sanj reminded Sylvie that the local community college had rolling, open admission.

"*Community* college," she said snidely.

"You can transfer somewhere better next year."

"I'm not going to college."

"Then lose the weight," Sanj said. "I don't understand why you didn't lose it in the first place. Ten pounds. That's nothing."

"It's easier for boys," she said.

They were in the wood-paneled rec room at Sylvie's, watching MTV's *120 Minutes*: two full hours devoted to alternative music videos—The Cocteau Twins, The Cure, Siouxsie and the Banshees—musicians never played on the pop rock station in their small town.

Sylvie's twin brother, Chris, had wandered through twice already, on his way to and from the kitchen. He was a football player. He was on the starting lineup, even though he wasn't very good. Chris wasn't very good at anything. His grades were appalling, one year so low he was disqualified from sports. He wasn't even particularly good-looking. But for some reason Sanj had secretly fallen for him. Maybe it was the way he padded around the house, always in sweatpants, always shirtless, regardless of the temperature outside, his muscles taut and toned. Maybe it was his curly hair, ringlets framing his face, and the rattail he grew in the back, unfashionable even then. To Sanj, part of what was seductive about Chris was the thought that this was the best time of his life. It wouldn't get any better. He wouldn't get better looking. He wasn't skilled enough to go further in football. He wasn't going to college. This was it for him. For Sanj, being around someone who was living the best years of his life, while Sanj was living perhaps the worst of his, was seductive.

Sylvie's was a sweatpants household. That's all Sanj had ever seen any of them wearing, at least at home. Sylvie was the exception. Even when she didn't need to be, she was stylish. Tonight she was wearing designer jeans and chandelier earrings.

Sylvie and Sanj had been outcasts in high school, each the other's only friend. They were proud of their status. As far as they were concerned, no one in the high school was worthy of their friendship.

In spring, they'd attended the senior prom together. ("Just as friends," Sylvie had said. Sanj hadn't told anyone he was gay, but he wondered if Sylvie had guessed.) Neither had particularly wanted to go, but Sylvie, at the last minute, had said, "What if we don't go and regret it for the rest of our lives?" Sanj instantly recognized that she was quoting the nerdy character from a teen soap that had been their Thursday-night guilty pleasure. He shot back, "What if we *do* go and regret it for the rest of our lives?" but in the end he relented. He was glad. At the prom, he was proud to have Sylvie on his arm. While the other girls wore tacky pastel confections, Sylvie wore couture. Well, not quite couture, but close: an emerald green Yves Saint Laurent cocktail dress she'd picked up on sale at Bergdorf, where she'd stopped after her interview at the modeling agency. It was an unbelievably extravagant expenditure for her, and she'd had to use all the money she'd saved over two years working part-time at the mall; even then, she'd had to charge the rest to her parents' credit card. But she'd thought of it as a reward, and reasoned that she would need such clothes for her new life in New York.

During an R.E.M. video—"It's the End of the World as We Know It (And I Feel Fine)"—Sylvie reached for Sanj's hand and said, "I can't believe you're leaving me here."

Sanj squeezed her hand and said, "I'll always be here for you."

Three days later, the day Sanj left for college, Sylvie came to say good-bye. He and his father were almost finished packing his new Jeep Cherokee—a graduation gift—which they would be driving together cross-country to L.A. They had a circular driveway, with a large fountain in the middle. Sanj's mother was perched on the front porch of the house supervising when Sylvie pulled up in her dented Toyota Tercel.

Sanj saw his mother's face before he saw Sylvie; he saw her jaw drop, her eyes widen, her arms fold tightly. She'd never liked Sylvie. She didn't like where Sylvie lived, or what she knew of Sylvie's brother and parents, not that she'd ever met them. She'd said as much to Sanj, as gently and tactfully as she could manage, coming to his room one evening as he was preparing to meet Sylvie. "Most people around here won't amount to much. We are not like them." She'd taken his chin in one hand. "Sanju, beta, find better friends."

Looking at Sylvie on their driveway, Sanj saw why his mother was clicking her tongue and shaking her head. The last time Sanj had seen Sylvie, her hair was long, luxurious, honey-blond, falling halfway down her back. Now she was completely bald.

Sanj didn't need to ask her why she'd done it. A few months ago, they'd watched an interview with Sinéad O'Connor on *120 Minutes*. She'd said that before she shaved her head, no one took her seriously; she was too pretty. Her decision, she said, had changed everything.

Sylvie walked up to Sanj and threw her arms around him. He pulled her close, stroking her bald head. "Your hair."

"We're both starting new lives," she said bravely, and for a moment he believed her. Then he noticed she was trembling.

"You'll get out of here, too. One day soon. I'll help you. I promise."

He didn't see Sylvie again for four years. During that time, he barely even spoke to her on the phone. When he first moved away, she called fairly often, leaving messages on the answering machine in his dorm room. He was always out. He rarely returned her calls.

They had drifted apart, it was natural. He didn't understand why they should pretend to be friends forever just because they had clung to each other during a few miserable years of high school.

So he wasn't quite prepared for what he saw when he ran into her in the pharmacy. It must have registered on his face. She had gained a little more weight, but that wasn't what threw him. Her whole being seemed to have changed. Whatever bright light had shone from her in high school was gone. She resembled neither the siren in the emerald green cocktail dress, nor the beautiful bald young woman Sanj had last seen. Now she wore gray sweatpants and a bulky, navy hooded sweatshirt emblazoned with the Mountaineers football logo. Her hair, long again, was pulled back in a ponytail. Sanj wouldn't have recognized her, wouldn't have thought to say hello, had she not approached him, saying his name timidly, tentatively. . . . *Sanj?*

"Sylvie?"

"It's great to see you."

"You, too," he said.

"Are you here long?"

"Just a couple of weeks," he said. "I'm taking care of my grandfather while my parents are in India." He held up the white paper bag from the pharmacy. "Heart medication."

"How's California?"

"I live in New York now. I work for *Vogue*." Sanj struck a pose from the Madonna "Vogue" video. He saw a flicker of pain flitter across her face. He'd forgotten she'd once dreamed of being photographed for such a magazine.

"I've only been here a few days. I'd been planning to call you," he said, though the truth was that he'd had no intention of getting in touch.

"I'm at the same number."

He said, "I'll call."

Sanj had only been living in New York for four months when his parents summoned him back to West Virginia to stay with his grandfather. At first he'd said no. "I can't take off just like that. I have a job."

"Internship," his mother corrected. "Unpaid. *Vogue* isn't paying you. Your parents are paying for you."

"Even so, I've made a commitment."

"He doesn't need to be taken care of," Sanj's mother said. "You won't have to do anything. I wouldn't even ask you, except I don't feel comfortable leaving him alone for so long." After a minute she said, "Don't make me beg."

Later, Sanj called her back. "Fine. Three weeks. That's it."

His parents were going to India to close up his grandmother's house in Rajkot, to sort through and sell her possessions, and to bring her to live in America for good. This was his mother's mother. The grandfather they wanted him to look after was his father's father, who had been living with them since Sanj was a child. His mother's mother didn't want to come. She didn't want to leave Rajkot to live—for the first time in her life at the age of seventy-eight—in America, in West Virginia, but Sanj's parents insisted she was too old to live alone.

Sanj wasn't exactly living in New York, not in the city anyway. He was living on Long Island with family friends. Chandu had been Sanj's father's childhood friend growing up in Gujarat in a village near Ahmedabad. They were like brothers. Chandu and Sanj's father, Bipin, had immigrated together to America at age seventeen. Literally *together*. Together, they had taken a bus from their village to Ahmedabad, a train from Ahmedabad to Bombay, a ship from Bombay to Spain, a train from Spain to London, a ship from London to New York, and finally, a Greyhound bus from New York to Oklahoma, where they were both enrolled, premed, at the university in Norman. (Later, Bipin told Sanj that his only ideas about Oklahoma, before arriving, were from the movie version of the musical.) Their journey took close to two months. Eventually, he and Chandu would attend different medical schools, do their residencies in different hospitals, settle in different regions, but they always kept in touch and saw each other as often as they could. Over the years, a surprising number of young men from their village ended up immigrating. Now, every four or five years, they'd have a big reunion, in rotating cities where one or the other lived, and everyone would bring their families. Sanj remembered one, years ago. He remembered in particular watching the men—soft in middle age—playing volleyball. They seemed so happy, like they were in the village again, like they were twelve.

Chandu's wife, Lala, didn't speak English, which made it difficult for Sanj to communicate with her, since he himself didn't speak any Indian languages. Almost thirty years she had been living in the United States, and she'd learned barely a handful of words and phrases. Sanj was shocked by this. True, Long Island had a vibrant Indian community, and Lala had plenty of people to talk to in her native languages. And true, Lala had never worked outside the house, and so she didn't need English for those purposes. But still, how had she passed her driver's exam? How did she manage while shopping?

Chandu and Lala had three daughters, all a few years older than Sanj. They all still lived at home. They were beautiful, with thick black hair. They were good Indian daughters: practical, responsible, accomplished. One was in med school, one was in law school, and one had just finished business school. Chandu seized every chance to brag about them.

The Princess Jasmine association wouldn't have occurred to Sanj, except that someone from Gita's MBA program told her she looked like her, from the Disney movie *Aladdin*. "Isn't that a little culturally insensitive?" Sanj had said at dinner. "Princess Jasmine isn't even Indian." But no one else thought so, and Gita liked the comparison. She thought it was flattering. Princess Jasmine was beautiful, even if she was just a cartoon. The more Sanj thought about it, the more he agreed: she did look like Princess Jasmine. In fact, all three sisters looked like Princess Jasmine. So, privately, that's what he started calling them: The Princess Jasmines, or sometimes just The Jasmines.

The Jasmines had the entire third floor of the house all to themselves. Each had her own bedroom and her own en suite bathroom. It smelled like hair products up there.

The parents' room was on the second floor, as was Sanj's. He stayed in what was usually the family's puja room, where they did their morning and evening prayers. There was a small mandir with statues and framed pictures of various gods. Sanj slept on a foldout futon.

He liked to sleep late. Mornings, the family members came in, one by one, whether or not Sanj was awake. If he woke up during their prayers, he would shuffle off to the bedroom of whichever Jasmine was already awake and climb into her empty bed to catch a few more minutes of sleep. The parents didn't like this, Sanj could tell. The father seemed particularly bothered. It was inappropriate, borderline scandalous. After all, Sanj was a young man, and these were young, unmarried women. The Jasmines didn't like it either. But no one was going to say anything. Sanj was the son of their father's dear childhood friend. They had traveled together in search of new lives in a new country, and together had weathered difficulties others could only imagine. A few transgressions from Bipin's only son could be overlooked.

The Jasmines hated New York. They thought it was dirty and crowded and expensive. They wanted to move to L.A. Sanj said L.A. was superficial. The Jasmines said New York was overrated. They narrowed their eyes. "You'll hate it here. You'll see."

Sylvie asked, "Do you still have that huge screen, with the projection television and the sprawling sectional?"

Three days after running into her at the pharmacy, Sanj had called and invited her over to watch a movie. She said she would bring the video.

When she arrived at the house, she rang the doorbell at the front door instead of the side door, where anyone who knew the family would have rung, and where Sylvie herself would have rung back in high school. Back then, Sylvie didn't even need to, she could just walk right in.

Sanj greeted her at the door, and, glimpsing the same dented Toyota Tercel, he remembered their good-bye in the driveway more than four years ago. Sanj invited Sylvie in.

The house's foyer was designed to impress. The ceilings were almost thirty feet high, and there was a five-foot-tall bronze statue of Nataraja Shiva, dancing his dance of destruction and re-creation. Sanj's parents had had it shipped from Chicago, along with other decorative items, including several large tapestries and an ornate indoor swing. They patterned their house after the fancy havelis in Bollywood films. The verandas in the back had floors of imported marble (as did the foyer) and ornate columns with gold-toned scrolls.

Bipin had been the first Indian to move to the small town. The job at the local hospital was the first one he'd been offered after his residency, and, eager to find a place where he could settle so he could bring his new bride from India, he'd taken it. Not long after, he decided to open his own oncology practice. When it was time for him to expand, he recruited an Indian. Then another. Other Indian doctors followed: family members, friends of friends. Word spread that there were opportunities in the area, and those who had nowhere else to go, who had Indian degrees and few options, began arriving. Most were doctors. Some were engineers, working in the chemical plants that dotted the river valley. Many of them lived with Bipin's family for a time—two, three weeks, sometimes longer—until they could find their own places and send for their wives and, in some cases, children. Bipin's family lived in a smaller house then, and the young men would sleep on a foldout in a room that doubled as Bipin's study. Now, thirty years later, there were more than twenty-five families. They were some of the wealthiest residents in what was otherwise a poor stretch of Appalachia.

Not only was Bipin the first Indian in town, he was also the first to buy land in Mulberry Hills, the first to build a house, custom-designed with a basement large enough to accommodate most, if not all, of the Indian community. This was useful, since Diwali celebrations could no longer be held in the recreation hall of the Episcopal Church, not since a janitor had told the deacon about the statue of the elephant-headed god, the chanting and dancing and burning of incense. Other Indian families followed, building several houses in a row. At Diwali and Holi and Navratri and at the monthly dandiya parties, the guests could easily hop from one house to the next. The Indians referred to Mulberry Hills as Malabar Hill, after the tony Bombay neighborhood.

The circular driveway and the accompanying fountain were added a few years after the house itself. Bipin had bought them for his wife as a surprise for their twentieth anniversary. Meenakshi had gone alone for a short trip to India, and when she returned—only half awake after the long journey—the driveway she pulled into was this one. The driveway itself was fairly simple; it was the fountain that was the real gift. It was exquisite. What made it so extraordinary, aside from its sheer size, were the hand-crafted tiles encircling its base. Most had standard decorative motifs Bipin had selected from a showroom: curlicues or geometric patterns or sunflowers. But scattered among them were a few very special tiles Bipin had commissioned to document his and Meenakshi's lives together—a tile with a mangalsutra exactly like the one Meenakshi had worn at their wedding; a tile depicting the Taj Mahal, where they had gone on their honeymoon; one with a baby's crib and the birth date of their only child; one with a palm tree to represent the trip to Hawai'i they had taken on their second anniversary, staying at an expensive resort, long before they had yet made the kind of money to afford such a vacation or resort, telling themselves the trip was an act of faith, a message to the universe that this was the kind of life they expected and that they would settle for nothing less.

Three years later, when the driveway needed to be repaired (long before it should have), Bipin, unable to secure the contractor who had originally built it, hired a local man. After the work was done, the two men argued, the local man demanding much more money than his original quote. The man got angry, shouting, "You foreigners don't know how hard it is. You all live in mansions. One day, come see where I live. Then you'll understand." Bipin ended up paying the man the extra money, though he continued to complain about it even years later.

Shortly after the driveway and fountain were built, Sanj's grandfather, getting into the car one day, said, "Life is a circle. One way or another we return to the beginning." The comment had irritated Sanj; it seemed to him both sentimental and false. In fact, it had become an inside joke between him and his parents. Bipin would imitate Sanj's grandfather in an exaggerated

Indian accent, stabbing the air with his finger, "Life is a circle," and Sanj and his mother would laugh. Though now, standing in the grand foyer with Sylvie, Sanj wondered if his grandfather hadn't had a point. After all, here Sanj was, four years after leaving, back where he started. But that was temporary. What Sanj hadn't mentioned to his grandfather, when his grandfather first made the observation, was that the driveway, though circular, did have an entrance, and, importantly, an exit, and Sanj had every intention of using it.

The first thing Sanj noticed about Sylvie when she stepped into the foyer was that she was wearing sweatpants again. She looked out of place, her sneakers ratty against the marble floor. She'd brought Krzysztof Kieslowski's *La Double Vie de Véronique*. Sanj had already seen it, but he didn't mind seeing it again. A professor had screened it in a film class in college. In the movie, Irène Jacob plays a double role: a Polish singer and a young French woman. The women never meet, yet for a time their lives seem to parallel one another's before eventually going off in different directions. Sanj remembered the professor having said something about the film being a moody exploration of identity, of free will versus destiny, but Sanj couldn't remember exactly. He'd earned a "C" in the course.

Sanj liked the soundtrack. Sylvie liked the styling: the clothes, the hair, the makeup. She was enthralled by Irène Jacob. "Fuck Julia Roberts," she said. "*This* is a star." The comment sounded just like something Sylvie might have said four years ago, and for a moment Sanj felt like they were back in high school. But then he glanced over at her—her shapeless sweats, her greasy hair—and remembered neither of them was the same.

The basement had a wet bar, and after the movie, Sanj made margaritas, and the two sat on the sectional, talking, watching

MTV on mute. Sylvie asked if he'd ever seen Anna Wintour.

"Of course. I've seen her several times in the halls and the lobby."

"I heard she had a skylight installed in her office so she can wear sunglasses even while she's at work."

"I've never been in her office. But once, in the elevator, she told me she loved my watch. 'It's Lucite,' I said. 'I have it in three colors.'"

A few minutes later Sanj said, "I love working at *Vogue*, but it's a little superficial."

Sanj noticed Sylvie's eyes welling up with tears. Her body crumpled, curling in on itself like a worm.

"Four years," Sylvie said. "Why didn't you call me? Why didn't you stop by? I thought we were best friends."

After a minute, she said, "These years have been really hard for me."

"I know," Sanj said.

"If you knew, you would have called."

Sanj remembered a night during their senior year in high school. It was February, and they had driven to Cleveland to see a Nine Inch Nails concert. In honor of the show, they were clad head-to-toe in black. It was midnight by the time the concert was finished and they started driving home. They'd gone in Sylvie's Tercel, and somehow they'd taken a wrong turn and ended up on a back road driving through farmland. Something Sanj said, he wasn't sure what—was it about the concert? about Nietzsche, whom they were both reading, and whom they had been discussing on and off during their drive?—upset Sylvie so much, she stopped the car and stepped out into the cold night without her coat, slamming the car door behind her. Sanj waited several minutes, wondering what to do, before finally getting out himself. Sylvie's back was turned to him. She was facing the field, her hands tightly gripping the fence. In the silence of the frigid night, Sanj could still hear the concert ringing in his ears. A cow was mooing somewhere in the distance. Sanj put his hand on Sylvie's shoulder and said, "I'm sorry," although he was unsure what he was apologizing for. He felt her shoulder beneath his hand soften and relax. They got back in the car and drove home without discussing it further.

Sanj tipped his margarita glass back, trying to get the last few sips. The ice cubes were cold against his lips. He set the glass down on the table and reached to put his hand on Sylvie's shoulder, to tell her he was sorry, as he had that night on the side of the road. But as he reached, he saw Sylvie's shoulder slightly, though perceptibly, pull away.

"I'll make it up to you," Sanj said. "Somehow. I promise."

Sanj was lying to everyone about what he was doing in New York. He didn't have an internship at *Vogue*. He didn't have an internship anywhere, not anymore. When he first arrived, he'd worked at a trade publication which served the prescription drug industry, and which he'd seen advertised on a flyer in the journalism office at USC. But he didn't last long.

In college, when Sanj had fantasized about his first job in New York, he'd pictured a spacious, light-filled office, with an open floor plan—no walls or cubicle barriers. He pictured himself wearing tight charcoal gray pants (wool, with a little bit of Lycra for stretch), a white shirt, and a skinny tie. He would share—with an equally stylish young woman, in a blue blouse, with short, ruffled sleeves—a large, antique table, and they would sit facing each other, gold-rimmed tea cups carefully positioned on coasters within easy reach. Occasionally, they'd look away from their work to exchange a clever comment about an art exhibit or a new dance club.

His real job, of course, was nothing like this. The office had drop ceilings and fluorescent lights. The job itself was tedious and uninspiring. Sanj was assigned to an editor and was responsible for sorting through his mail, screening his phone calls, and typing and sending his handwritten correspondence to freelance writers.

His boss had a ridiculous name—Jeep—made all the more ridiculous by how poorly it suited him. Far from rugged or virile, Jeep was stout and fey. "I had a Jeep," Sanj said, the first day, "but I totaled it on the way back from Burning Man." He thought Jeep would find this anecdote funny and that it would break the ice; instead, Jeep just shrugged.

Jeep had only been at the trade publication for six months. Before that, he'd been a senior culture editor at *Newsday*, but he'd been pushed out during a restructuring. For Jeep, the job at the trade magazine was a huge step down, something Sanj understood almost immediately. Jeep mentioned *Newsday* at least twenty times Sanj's first day. In his previous position, Jeep had also had his own assistant. Here, he'd have to settle for an intern.

Among Sanj's duties was fetching Jeep's lunch—a different place every day—so Sanj, still trying to learn the lay of the neighborhood, often found himself lost. Jeep always paid Sanj after Sanj returned, not before. Sanj wondered if Jeep didn't trust him with the money. One afternoon, during Sanj's second week, Jeep sent him out for a turkey sandwich. When the man behind the counter asked if he wanted mustard, Sanj didn't know. He couldn't remember. Had Jeep said anything about mustard? To be safe, Sanj ordered two sandwiches—one with mustard, one without—deciding that he would allow Jeep to select the one he wanted and that Sanj would eat the other himself. Back at the office, after Jeep selected the sandwich without mustard, he forgot to pay Sanj, and Sanj couldn't think of a polite way to ask. Later, sitting alone in the break room, Sanj couldn't stop thinking about the money. His internship wasn't even paid, and now he had to buy his boss's lunches? On top of everything, the sandwich left a bad taste in his mouth. He hated mustard.

The next day, Jeep sent Sanj to a sushi restaurant on Twenty-eighth Street, again without any money. Sanj ordered the sashimi lunch his boss had requested. At the last minute, he amended the order—"To stay, not to go"—and, sitting on a stool at a long table facing the street, he ate the sashimi himself, savoring the delicate fish, relishing it even more knowing that Jeep would go hungry this afternoon. After finishing, instead of returning to the office, Sanj walked crosstown to Penn Station to catch a train back to Long Island. He never went back to work, never even called to explain his absence, and Jeep, to Sanj's surprise, never called Sanj in Long Island to find out why he'd disappeared.

Sanj knew his parents wouldn't pay for him to live in New York unless they thought he was working, so he didn't tell anyone he'd quit. To explain to his parents why they could no longer reach him at the work number he had originally given them, he told them he'd found a better internship at *Vogue*. When they asked for the new number, he explained that the editors there were very hierarchical. "I don't even have my own desk, let alone a phone."

Every day, Sanj would take the Long Island Rail Road to Penn Station, and then he'd kill time in the city until it was a respectable hour to return home. Some days he'd walk over to the Mid-Manhattan Public Library, and he'd read the papers, looking for possible employment. Other days, he would take the subway to various neighborhoods and walk around, trying to orient himself to New York.

Sometimes he'd wander around with a handheld tape recorder, and he would approach random people, claiming he was working on an article about this or that for *GQ* or the *New York Post* or *Paper* magazine. He was having a tough time in New York. If he could better understand the minds of New Yorkers, he reasoned, maybe he could figure out how to live in this city. Besides, he had no friends and was starving for conversation. On Forty-second Street, he asked pedestrians what they thought of the haikus an artist had installed on the marquees of the derelict porn theaters. Another time, on a particularly bleak stretch of the Meatpacking District, he asked people what they thought the city should do to beautify the neighborhood. "How about a park?" he'd suggested. "Don't you ever wish you had more green in your lives?" Part of what amazed Sanj was how quick people were to believe he was who he said he was. No one ever seemed to doubt him.

One day, wandering around Times Square, Sanj noticed, next to a Howard Johnson, a steep stairway with an awning that read, "Gaiety Theatre." Sanj remembered seeing a small ad in the back of the *Village Voice*. It featured a naked male torso—slender and smooth—with the words, "Male Burlesk."

He climbed the stairs and paid the cover admission. Inside was a large room with small tables and a stage where the striptease took place. Most of the customers, at least this weekday afternoon, were businessmen dressed in suits, taking a long lunch or an afternoon break from the office. Or so Sanj assumed. Maybe they weren't businessmen. Maybe they were like Sanj: pretending. Pretending to be businessmen, pretending to have jobs they went to every day.

The strippers were pretending, too, though, of course this was their job: to pretend to be soldiers or airline pilots or gang-banging thugs or firefighters. They were all different. Some were thick with gym-won muscles. Others were wiry. Some were out-of-work models and actors and dancers. Sanj thought he recognized one of the dancers from Madonna's Blond Ambition Tour, which he'd seen when it aired live on HBO. Some were strung-out junkies. This particular afternoon, there was also a guest headliner, a porn star. Sanj had seen one of his videos in college and already knew what the man looked like naked, somewhat spoiling the tease part of the striptease. But it was more than made up for by the excitement Sanj felt being near someone he'd seen onscreen having sex.

The end of each striptease was always the same. When the performer got down to his G-string, he would disappear backstage, music still playing, and then reemerge completely naked, with an erection. Sometimes he emerged quickly. Sometimes he was backstage for a very long time, trying to get hard.

When he returned to the stage, his penis erect, he wouldn't dance; his erection was an encumbrance. Instead, he'd sort of saunter, and then he would pick a customer and walk right up to him, standing inches from him, hands on his hips, pelvis thrust forward, like Superman, his dick right in the customer's face. The customers knew they weren't supposed to touch. The stripper just stood like this: motionless, smiling, the customer staring at his crotch. If there was time, the stripper would go around to two or three or four customers and stand in front of them one at a time. Sanj could tell he was choosing men he thought might be interested in hiring him out later, men who seemed old or closeted. The stripper could only stay onstage as long as his erection lasted. Once his dick reached four o'clock, he would disappear behind the curtain.

Sanj liked imagining what went on backstage, what the performers had to do to get aroused. Was someone helping them? A boyfriend? A girlfriend? Another stripper? Or was there a special employee whose whole job was to aid them with their erections? Hadn't Sanj heard of that? Wasn't it called a fluffer? What images did the men rely upon? What fantasies, what private desires? Sanj wished he could crack their heads open and see. Oddly, his favorite part of the whole show wasn't when the men were visible, but when they had disappeared backstage, and the crowd was waiting for them to reemerge. He loved the anticipation.

Sanj returned to the Gaiety many times. Once, he even tried to interview one of the performers: a British guy, who, during his act, had worn a G-string with a Union Jack on the crotch. Sanj found him in the small, adjoining lounge where the strippers would sometimes loiter afterward, hoping to pick up tricks. Claiming to be from *Genre* magazine, Sanj had thrust his tape recorder into the man's face. "What were you thinking about backstage to get hard?" Pushing the tape recorder aside, the man winked and said, "You."

Lala, Chandu's wife, had her suspicions about Sanj. There were days he didn't wake until noon, didn't leave for the train until two. She didn't know much about internships, about the working world of Manhattan, but she knew enough to recognize that there wasn't a job on earth that would let you show up whenever you happened to feel like it, not a job this boy could get anyway.

And then there were days he didn't take the train into the city at all. He'd claim he was going to work, but instead he'd put on his Walkman and embark on long walks, returning sometimes two or three hours later. She knew because once she saw him from her car while running errands. He was just standing in front of a Carvel, less than a mile from their house, headphones on, gazing in the shop window.

Lala remembered when she first arrived in America—when her husband was working long hours at the hospital and before her daughters were born or she learned to drive—she, too, would go for long walks. Her mind would often drift back to Ahmedabad, back to some typical scene from childhood, like the view of the Sabarmati River from her bedroom window, or the dosa shop her family would visit on Saturdays, or the crowded, narrow streets of the Old City, the jumble of scooters and camels and cows. Then she'd look at her watch and suddenly realize three hours had passed, and she was in a public park she didn't recognize, sitting on a bench, watching a blond couple playing with a puppy in the grass under a grove of oaks, and she'd wonder, "How have I ended up here?" Sometimes she saw in the boy's eyes, when he'd returned from his walks, that same lost look.

Yes, there was something she liked about Sanj. These days, her daughters were all busy with school or their first jobs. She saw them only in the evenings, and even then they seemed to come home later and later. She was grateful for Sanj's company.

One morning when she was vacuuming, and her back, which caused her chronic pain, was particularly achy, the boy—at the table pouring a bowl of cereal—noticed. Without either of them saying a word, he gently took the vacuum handle from her and finished the work. Since then, twice a week he ran the vacuum without being asked.

There were smaller things, too. On nights when he came home very late—which happened often—entering the house long after everyone was asleep, he tiptoed so quietly, no one ever woke up. Lala would leave a plate of leftovers for him, whatever the family had eaten for dinner that night. She'd set the plate and a glass of milk on the kitchen table under a small tabletop mosquito net she'd bought in India on one of her annual visits. Each morning, she'd find the dishes, the glass, the cutlery all carefully washed and dried and put away in the cupboards. Such a small thing, yet she loved this about him. This back and forth—her leaving the food out each night, his washing and putting away the dishes for her to find the next morning—felt like a private communication between them, their only communication, since they shared no languages.

Once, when Lala had invited three ladies over to the house to prepare sweets for an upcoming holy function, the boy sat down with them at the kitchen table and sliced almonds into paper-thin slivers, thinner than any of the women could slice. When Neela looked at him sideways, and said, "Lala, three daughters on their way out of the house, but no matter: you have found a fourth daughter," and the other ladies giggled, Lala was glad the boy didn't understand Gujarati.

One morning, when Sanj was toasting bread in his parents' kitchen in West Virginia, he noticed his grandfather hovering. Several times, he seemed to start to speak to Sanj, but he couldn't quite form the words, and Sanj did nothing to make it easier. Sanj had never felt close to his grandfather. He was, at best, a vague and ghostly presence in Sanj's life.

After several false starts, his grandfather said, "Sanju, beta, tell me about your life in New York."

Why was his grandfather asking? Sanj wondered. Besides, what was there to tell? What could his grandfather possibly understand about his life?

"I'm working," Sanj said. When his grandfather seemed to want more, Sanj added, "At a magazine."

"What kind of magazine?"

"Fashion."

Again his grandfather struggled to find words, before asking, "Are you happy?"

Sanj didn't know how to answer. "Were you happy? When you were young and just starting out? Were you happy?"

His grandfather thought for a minute, then said, "It was a different time. I had different responsibilities."

Sanj remembered, when he was ten, visiting the house in India where his grandfather lived and where his father was born. It was his one and only trip to India. He and his parents had taken a local bus forty minutes from Ahmedabad to the village. Children had followed them from the bus station, through the dusty lanes, all the way to the house. The structure itself was dilapidated, with a badly cracked façade and a trash-strewn entryway. Several families shared it. Sanj's grandfather's flat consisted of just two small rooms upstairs. But no one from the family had lived there for twenty years, and no one knew who lived there now. Pointing to the dark window upstairs, Sanj's mother said, "Can you believe your father is from there?" and, in fact, Sanj could not.

Speaking with his grandfather now, Sanj realized that when his father was born, his grandfather must not have been much older than Sanj currently was. He considered the sacrifices his grandparents must have made to get his father out of that village, to send their son to America. The fare alone must have required months, if not years, of careful saving.

"I know fashion may sound frivolous," Sanj said, "but it's a very famous magazine. Anyone would want this job. My friends can't believe how lucky I am."

After that first night, watching *La Double Vie de Véronique* in Sanj's basement, Sylvie and Sanj saw each other every day, sometimes twice. Mostly they watched movies at Sanj's, downing margaritas or daiquiris or vodka tonics. From the stories Sylvie told, Sanj pieced together that she had taken classes at the community college, but had only lasted one semester. He learned she had spent much of the last year doing what his parents were doing in India now: helping to clean out the apartment of her mother's mother, who had been terminally ill, and who had died just two months earlier.

One evening, Sylvie asked Sanj to meet her at her house. Sanj hadn't been to Sylvie's since high school. It was only a couple of miles from where he lived, just down the hill in the jumble of small houses crowded in the narrow valley close to the riverbank, in the part of town that flooded when it rained too much. Sylvie's house was a compact, two-story structure that looked neglected, with peeling blue paint and a sagging front porch. A stone goose stood sentry on the front lawn; Sylvie's mom liked to dress it according to the weather and the season—a yellow slicker when it rained, earmuffs in the winter, a red Santa hat around Christmas. Today had been beautiful, and the goose was wearing sunglasses.

Sanj knocked on the door that entered into the kitchen. Sylvie's father swung the door open and shook Sanj's hand. The kitchen was small, with a linoleum floor that needed replacing, and a floral curtain-rod ruffle over the window above the sink. The kitchen radio was set to an oldies station. Sylvie's mother was standing at the counter, chopping carrots. She turned to Sanj. "We haven't seen you in forever! Look at you!" Sanj noticed right away that they were both wearing sweatpants, just as he'd remembered them. They looked older, though, more so than the four years that had elapsed. Sylvie's mother came toward him, her arms open, and hugged him.

Sanj saw Sylvie, who had been lurking in the doorway. She came over to him, grasped his hand, and pulled him away from her mother, whom he was still embracing. At first, her mother looked hurt, but then she resumed her work at the kitchen counter. As Sylvie dragged him into the hallway, Sanj thought he saw someone sitting on the couch in the other room watching television.

Upstairs, Sylvie's door was shut and locked. It was a heavy bolt lock, the kind you would find on the front door of a house, not an inside bedroom. Sylvie fished a key out of her sweatpants' pocket.

Her bedroom looked nothing like Sanj remembered. In high school, the room had been decorated with dingy wallpaper, some country theme, cornflowers perhaps, Sanj couldn't remember exactly. Not that you could see the wallpaper. Almost every inch had been covered with posters or pictures clipped from magazines: bands Sylvie liked, models she admired, fashions she hoped to one day wear. He remembered, in particular, above her bed, a poster of Morrissey looking both sullen and seductive.

Now her room was stripped of all that, stripped, it seemed, of Sylvie, or at least the Sylvie that Sanj had known. The room was austere. The matted, beige wall-to-wall carpeting had been ripped up, leaving roughly finished hardwood floors. The walls and the door were painted blue, and the trim around the windows was green. Pushed against one of the walls was a narrow wooden bed made up with a scarlet blanket of rough wool. There were two straight-backed wooden chairs with straw seats. Arranged on a small wooden table in the corner of the room were a blue pitcher and a blue washbasin and a drinking glass. Three blue shirts—men's shirts, from what Sanj could tell—hung on pegs along the back wall, and next to them, a straw hat. Everything about the room seemed odd to Sanj—unlikely, yet somehow familiar. It evoked another time and place.

Sylvie gestured for Sanj to sit on one of the chairs, which proved uncomfortable, while she took a seat on the other.

"You've redecorated your room," Sanj said.

"It's Van Gogh's."

It took Sanj a moment to understand. Then he remembered the painting—*Van Gogh's Room in Arles*—which was famous, and which he'd seen at the Art Institute in Chicago one summer when he was visiting his cousins.

"Why?" Sanj said.

"I don't know. I guess I felt a connection."

"A connection to the monastic atmosphere, or to the desperate guy who sliced off his ear?"

"Both."

He wondered, too, about the locks—what was it she was trying to keep out? or was it something she was trying to keep *in*?—but he didn't ask.

"Was that Chris I saw downstairs?"

"Probably," she said. "He's back again."

"What's he been up to?" Sanj asked, trying to sound casual, though he was eager to know.

"He had a baby with Trisha Meyers, but they're not together anymore. He installs car stereos. Ironic, since he lost his driver's license. DUI. He'd been smoking pot that night, but believe me, when it comes to drugs, that's the least of what he does. *Did? Does?* I don't even know anymore. I asked recently, and he said he was clean, but I don't believe him. There was a time when we could never lie to each other. We were so close: we're twins, after all. But that time is long gone."

The room was very quiet. They could hear beneath them, through the thin floor, the faint sounds from the kitchen: the oldies station ("All the leaves are brown . . ."), kitchen cabinets slamming, dishes being stacked. Sylvie said, "Let's not talk about Chris anymore. It makes me tired." In fact, the story was all too familiar, echoed in the lives of countless other young men they'd known in high school.

Sanj said, "I got a call from one of the *Vogue* editors today. I might get to write a piece. Well, really just a blurb, maybe three or four hundred words. But it's exciting nonetheless, partly because the story was my idea. See, I know this guy in L.A., a graffiti artist, a friend of a friend. He recently sold his novel. It won't be out until next year, but I pitched the article as a 'next big thing' piece. No one knows about him now, but this time next year everyone will be talking about him."

Sylvie smiled. "I'm happy for you," she said, though her eyes said otherwise. Sanj heard a tightness in her voice as she continued. "It seems like things have come easily for you since high school. First USC, now New York. Not that you haven't worked for it, or that you don't deserve it. It just seems to have been easy for you. Not for me." She leaned forward. "Why do you think that is?"

At first, Sanj wasn't sure if it was a rhetorical question, or if Sylvie expected a response.

After a minute, he said, "I've been lucky."

Sylvie sighed. "Lucky."

The sun was setting. The light in the room was fading; they were almost sitting in the dark.

She stood up. "Let's go downstairs. Maybe Chris will be gone."

Sanj's parents called every two or three days to check on him and his grandfather. When they'd call, it was morning in India, but evening in America, and Sanj would often be out. His grandfather would leave scribbled messages.

On the days Sanj did talk to his parents, he reassured them about his grandfather. "He's fine. You know him. He spends all day shut up in his bedroom doing puja." Sanj's mother would want to know about food. "Is it lasting?" Before leaving for India, she'd cooked nonstop for days, and filled the freezer. "If you run out, you can always call any of the aunties to bring something."

Sanj was on his way out the door to meet Sylvie when his father rang. "How's it going?" Bipin asked. "How's your grandfather?"

"Fine," Sanj said. "What about over there?"

"It's been tough for everyone, especially for your grandmother. She knows she'll probably never return here, not to this house anyway. Sorting through all her belongings has dredged up years' worth of memories, which hasn't made it any easier."

After a minute, Sanj's father said, "Do you remember that card you made for Dada when he was in the hospital? You must have been ten. You drew a carnival, remember, with a Ferris wheel, bumper cars, a shooting game with cartoon ducks? You raided the photo album, cutting out the heads of all your cousins, aunts, and uncles to paste on all the bodies you drew, even on the ducks. Your mom was so mad; they were the only copies of the photos. Dada was so proud, he showed it to all the nurses and doctors at the hospital. Your grandmother kept that card all these years."

Sanj had forgotten about the card, though he had a vivid memory of the trip to India a few weeks later, after his grandfather died. It was the same trip when he'd visited his father's village.

"I remember seeing the house where you were born," Sanj said.

"I went there over the weekend," Bipin said. "Just for the day. Just to look around again."

Visiting the village, Bipin had had his own flood of memories. He had thought about the day he left for America, meeting up with his friend Chandu that morning. Chandu's mother had made them hot paranthas and potato vegetable, and even though

Bipin had eaten breakfast at his own house just half an hour earlier, he ate again.

The journey had been exhausting. He remembered in particular an incident during their stopover in Paris. Chandu and the two other Indian men with whom they'd been traveling wanted to go to a burlesque show. "Paris is famous for them," they'd said. Bipin said he had a stomachache. In truth, he felt awkward about going. It seemed somehow wrong, although, even after the men left, there was a small part of Bipin that wished he'd gone, not just for the titillation, but also because he wished he were the type of man who would go: adventuresome, fearless. Instead, he stayed in the hotel and wrote his father a long letter thanking him for the sacrifices he'd made to send him to America, assuring him that they wouldn't be for nothing. "I'll make you proud," he'd written. When he went to the post office, he got flummoxed, struggling to understand the French system, and ended up never mailing the letter, pocketing it instead and carrying it with him to America. Months later, he ran across it while sorting through some things. It was the end of his first year in college. Reading the letter, he was struck with homesickness, and he wanted so desperately to go back to India, if not for good, at least for a long summer visit. But he had no money. In fact, it would be another six years before he'd set foot in India, before he'd see any of his family. Bipin spent days moping in his room, refusing to come out.

It was Chandu who had rescued him. He organized a summer sublet, a large Victorian house in disrepair, which he and Bipin would share with four other foreign students who also had nowhere to go. In exchange for free rent, the men would fix up the house so the owner could sell it at the end of the summer.

That first night in the house, Chandu prepared a Gujarati feast. Well, not quite a feast, but Chandu had done the best he could with what ingredients he could find locally and with what limited cooking skills he possessed. Still, Bipin was impressed. He wondered where Chandu had learned to cook. Eating the food, Bipin swelled with memories of home, understanding, too, that as long as Chandu was there with him, he wasn't alone.

Bipin had never told his son this story. There was so much he'd never said. He'd never told him how many days he'd cried in Oklahoma; or how scared he was, when he brought Meenakshi to America, that he would disappoint her or fail her somehow; or how much he'd struggled. What Bipin *did* tell his son about his early life in America is what he thought he needed to know: that he had come with nothing and that it hadn't been easy, but he had worked hard and now here they all were. When Sanj asked his father *why* he came to America, Bipin answered, "For a better life," which was, in Bipin's estimation, what they now had. As for the details of what he'd been through, why would his son want to know? Bipin barely wanted to know himself.

Toward the end of their phone conversation, Sanj mentioned he'd been seeing quite a bit of his old friend Sylvie. "You remember Sylvie Pearson, right?"

"Of course," Bipin said. "You two were best friends."

When Sanj said he was eager to return to New York, Bipin said, "I'm glad Chandu Uncle is looking after you. I can't imagine how I would have survived in America without him. I don't know how either one of us could have survived."

The next time Sylvie came over, they watched *Sid & Nancy*. It had been one of their favorite movies when they were in high school. They were watching a scene in which Sid and Nancy are lying in a bed in the Chelsea Hotel, barely functional after shooting heroin. As Sid passes out, his lit cigarette accidentally singes Nancy, and she flicks it into a pile of rubbish on the ground—discarded clothes, empty fast-food containers, the crumpled wrapper of a Burger King Whopper—which catches fire. Instead of extinguishing it, Nancy merely watches the blaze, her eyes half-closed, as she curls her body against Sid's. Sid awakens, lights another cigarette, flicks the match into the growing fire. Neither of them does anything to save themselves.

Sanj paused the movie.

"What's wrong?" Sylvie asked.

He wanted to tell her the truth. He wanted to tell her he didn't work at *Vogue* and that his grades at USC had been dismal. He wanted to tell her he wasn't lucky, as he'd claimed in her bedroom (as he'd claimed to his grandfather, too), at least not lucky in the way she thought. He looked at her. The light of the television was blue on her face, though the fire on the screen was yellow and red.

He couldn't say it.

"Would you like more vodka?"

"Sure," Sylvie said. He got up to fix two more drinks. When he returned, handing Sylvie hers, he tried again to tell her, but said instead, "Let's toast."

"To what?" she asked.

He held up his glass. "To the future."

"To the future," Sylvie repeated, though her voice sounded more hesitant than Sanj's. Her eyes looked away as they clinked glasses.

He pushed play. The scene resumed. The firefighters break down the door, dragging Sid and Nancy, against their will, to safety. In the doorway, Nancy looks back at the inferno with longing.

Sanj had heard rumors about a gay bar: a place called Diff'rent Strokes. It was located in the deserted downtown, under a highway overpass. It was next door to a biker bar, about which he'd also heard rumors: a woman could get a free drink if she gave the bartender her bra to hang on the wall, two drinks if she gave up her panties. The biker bar and the gay bar had abutting parking lots and back-door entrances.

He had to show his ID and pay a dollar and sign a registry. The bar was technically "members only" ever since there was a stabbing a few months earlier. Sanj looked at the names above his to see if he recognized anyone, perhaps someone he had heard whispers about growing up: the newspaper editor, the math teacher, the chef at the French restaurant. Sanj was nervous about signing his name. What if someone he knew saw it afterward?

Inside, the space was dark and narrow, dominated by a long bar with stools. The floors and walls and ceilings were painted black. There was a tiny dance floor and two pool tables that seemed smaller than regulation size. Besides Sanj, there were only six or seven other people, mostly middle-aged men, no one Sanj would be interested in. They didn't seem particularly interested in him, either. Sanj knew they wanted rednecks in pickup trucks, not skinny little Indians. Sanj knew it, because that's who he wanted, too. He stayed almost two hours. The crowd didn't improve much, though at one point it peaked at about twenty. He shot one game of pool, though mostly he just sat at the bar.

Toward the end of the night, Sanj found himself talking to a guy who had come late and had sat next to him, a man in his late twenties or perhaps early thirties. He was cute, and he wore a red baseball cap pulled low on his head. He introduced himself as Chad. Sanj thought he recognized him, but wasn't sure. Sanj flirted with him. He took his baseball cap and put it on his own head. When Chad leaned in to retrieve it, Sanj kissed him long and hard. He whispered, "Take me home." Chad said, "I can't."

Driving home afterward, Sanj remembered him: Chad *Webster*. His house was near Sylvie's. He was a few years older than they were; in fact, Sanj remembered Sylvie saying he'd been her babysitter when she was a kid. Sanj remembered seeing him once, a few years ago, washing his car in the driveway—a sleekly beautiful '69 Dodge Charger, plum-colored. At the time, Sanj had fantasized about riding in the passenger seat, driving into the horizon with Chad's arm around him.

The next time Sanj talked to Sylvie, he asked about Chad.

"He went off to D.C. right after high school. He lived there several years, but then he got sick. He's been sick for a while. 'He's come home to rest.' That's what his mom told my mom. Why are you asking?"

"No reason," Sanj said. "I saw him in line at Foodland. He looked familiar, then I remembered he was your neighbor. I was just curious."

At home that night, Sanj couldn't stop thinking about Chad. *Sick?*

A few days before Sanj had left New York, he'd gone out to a bar in Chelsea. Soon after arriving, he downed three vodka tonics. Much of the night was a haze. A man groped him by the pay phones outside the bathroom. He'd introduced himself as Paul. He was accompanied by a young Indian man named Asher, who lived with his parents in Queens and was a med-school student, though apparently he was on the verge of failing out. Paul kept telling Sanj he and Asher were "just friends."

When Paul was getting them drinks, Asher took Sanj aside and said, "Paul and I used to be a couple. We're going through a rough patch, but he still loves me and I still love him. As a fellow Indian, you would never want to come between us. I'm trusting you. You are my brother."

Outside, Paul put Asher in a cab headed for Queens, and

he put his arm around Sanj and said, "Let's go." His place was nearby. It was a large, loft-style apartment, beautifully decorated. Sanj recognized the black chaise longue as a Le Corbusier. In bed, when Paul started to enter Sanj, Sanj asked, "Where's the condom?" Paul said, "We don't need it. I'm clean." When Sanj tried to push Paul away, Paul said, "C'mon." He kissed Sanj on the mouth then said, "It doesn't feel as good with one of those things on. It kills all the sensation." Sanj said, "Fine, but if you come inside me, I'll kill *you*."

Afterward, it was too late to catch a train back to Long Island. Lying next to Paul, Sanj couldn't sleep. He felt guilty for betraying Asher, not that he'd actually promised him anything. But more than that, Sanj couldn't believe, knowing all that he knew, that he'd let Paul fuck him without a condom. Sanj lay awake the next few hours, imagining Paul's fluids, *infected* fluids, Sanj imagined—a few drops of come or pre-come—invading his body. He imagined he could actually feel it: tiny cells of Paul— a complete stranger Sanj wouldn't even recognize were he to see him again—coursing through Sanj's body, up his torso, down through his arms and hands, up through his neck, the liquid pooling in his head in the hollows just behind his eyes. It was like Paul was a part of him now.

At five, Sanj got out of bed and left, Paul still asleep. He slogged onto the A train to Penn Station, waited half an hour for the next train, changed at Jamaica, walked the twenty minutes from his stop in Long Island to his uncle and auntie's house. The shops along the main street were just beginning to pull up their metal shutters. When he arrived at the house, Lala Auntie was in the kitchen in her nightgown and dressing coat, scraping into the garbage the food from the plate she had left out for Sanj the night before. She barely looked at him as he walked past her.

Sylvie's words about Chad echoed in Sanj's head: *He's come home to rest*. Sanj realized he needed to leave. Now. His parents were due back in just a few more days, but Sanj couldn't wait. He had to get out while he still could. He thought of the visit to Sylvie's a few days earlier: the sagging porch, the buckling linoleum floor, everyone in sweatpants. He remembered the promise he'd made to her four years ago, when he'd said, "You'll get out of here, too. I'll help you." He thought, too, of what his father had said on the phone about Chandu Uncle and their early years in America, how neither of them could have made it without the other. He decided that, this time, he wouldn't leave Sylvie behind.

Sylvie didn't need much convincing. She told her parents she was going on a week's vacation with Sanj, though she and Sanj—in words whispered to one another, as though saying them too loudly might jeopardize or jinx them—both hoped it would turn into something more. Aside from occasional trips across the river to Ohio, she hadn't set foot outside West Virginia since high school. She was ready for an adventure.

They took a cab to the bus station, a bus to Charleston, and a train from there to New York. The train would take twelve hours overnight.

In the row in front of them were a large woman and her young daughter, who must have been about eight and who was clutching a Bart Simpson doll. Across from them was an out-of-work coal miner—muscular and compact, with dirty fingernails. He was planning to show up, without forewarning, at the New Jersey house of his half-brother, with whom the man had never been particularly close. But he had nowhere else to go, or so he explained, over the course of a couple hours, to the large woman across the aisle. "I tried calling, Lord knows I tried. But I could never finish dialing. Partly because I was worried he'd say no, and then where would I go? But mostly because I'm just so embarrassed for screwing everything up." Later, he said to the woman, "You're so easy to talk to. Why can't everyone be like you?"

Sitting behind Sanj and Sylvie were preteen boys on their way back home to the Bronx (reluctant to be returning—"The Bronx is *tough*"—after having spent the summer with their aunt in South Carolina). As Sanj passed their seat on his way back from the toilet, he thought he'd heard one of them mutter "faggot," but wasn't sure. Later, the same boy popped his head over the seat, and asked Sanj if he could borrow the batteries from Sanj's Walkman to use in his own Walkman, and Sanj, for reasons he couldn't understand—given what he'd thought he'd heard the boy say earlier—complied. The boy blasted Tupac, sharing the earphones with his brother, listening through one speaker while his brother listened through the other.

It was night. Most of the lights in the train car were off, but many passengers hadn't pulled their curtains shut, and Sanj could see the lights from the streetlamps outside roll across Sylvie's face. The half-light gave everything in the compartment a dreamlike quality.

Sanj heard giggling, then moaning from the seat in front of him. When he ventured a peek, he saw that the man and the little girl had switched places. The man was now in the seat with the large woman, the woman's daughter sitting by herself across the aisle. Sanj saw the man on top of the woman, one hand over her breast, the other under her skirt. Sanj thought about the man's dirty fingernails.

Sanj and Sylvie slumped down in their chairs, their knees pressing against the seat in front of them. Sylvie whispered, "I want this to work. I want a new start." Sanj took her hand. She rested her head on his shoulder. In the dark car, cocooned among these people all coupled off—the man and the woman in the seat ahead, the boys sharing the earphones behind them, the little girl across the aisle hugging her Bart Simpson doll—Sanj felt the train tracks rumbling below him, the train car hurtling forward, and he felt hopeful, like they were heading toward something.

Early the next morning, groggy-eyed, they switched trains at Penn Station, and hopped on the LIRR to Long Island. Chandu was waiting for them at the stop.

Sanj hadn't told him he'd be bringing a friend, much less a *female* friend. Chandu Uncle looked surprised, then disappointed, shaking his head, but he didn't protest. At the house, The Jasmines gave Sylvie the once-over, their lips curling in disapproval as they tossed their perfumey hair. Only Lala showed any sympathy. Speaking to Meghana in a firm tone Sanj hadn't heard before, she arranged for Sylvie to share Meghana's bedroom. She also managed to teach Sylvie, through a series of gestures, how to eat Indian food properly, how to tear the roti with only one hand and to use it to scoop up the vegetables.

Still, Sanj could tell, almost immediately, it was a bad idea to have brought Sylvie. Whatever courage or resolve she had managed to muster in the dark on the train had quickly vanished. Instead, she retreated into herself. She didn't want to leave the house. When she did venture out—Sanj dragging her through SoHo ("This is the newsstand where I saw Naomi Campbell buying three copies of a magazine with her face on the cover; doesn't her manager provide her with copies?")—she lagged behind, barely looking up from the sidewalk.

By the third night, Sylvie had given Meghana the emerald green Yves Saint Laurent cocktail dress which she had bought at Bergdorf four years ago, and which she had packed for the trip, not out of any rational belief that she would be able to wear it again, that she would be able to fit into it or have the life that would warrant it, but out of a hope she was too frightened to even fully imagine or name. When Meghana, cooing over the dress, asked with disbelief, "This was *yours*?" Sylvie replied, "No, it belonged to someone else."

By then, Sanj's parents had returned from India with his grandmother. He spoke to them on the phone. His father told him about his briefcase, which had been stolen at JFK ("I only set it down for a minute in the restroom") and about his grand-mother, who had pouted the whole way and had barely spoken a word since arriving. "She's miserable," Bipin admitted. "But that's to be expected. It takes time."

Toward the end of the conversation, Bipin said, "You shouldn't have left your grandfather alone."

"He didn't need me."

"How do you know?"

Sanj had resumed his charade of pretending to go to work at *Vogue*, leaving Sylvie, most afternoons, alone with Lala. One day, he said, "Great news! They're letting me write the preview after all, the one about the emerging writer."

"I know," Sylvie said.

"How could you know? I just found out myself."

"No," Sylvie said. "I *know*."

"Know what?"

"The truth."

"About what?"

"Everything." She was looking directly at him, something, Sanj now realized, she rarely did. He noticed, too, for the first time, her eyes: emerald, like the dress, and glowing.

Sanj said, "You'll have to be more specific."

"I know why you were asking about Chad Webster."

Sanj didn't respond.

"I know you're gay."

"No shit, Sherlock."

"I know you don't work at *Vogue*." She looked to Sanj for a response, but he was quiet. It was he, now, who was averting his eyes. She said, "You're not fooling anyone."

"My parents . . ."

"Your parents," she said, interrupting, "don't *want* to know the truth."

He wondered how she knew about *Vogue*, and for how long she'd known. Had she known sitting on the sectional in his basement, watching *La Double Vie de Véronique*, when he told her about Anna Wintour and the Lucite watches? Or when they sat together in the Van Gogh room? Had she listened to him rattle on and on about the article he'd pitched, knowing he was making it all up? When he'd said he was lucky, was she secretly laughing at him? *Lucky, my ass.*

"You're jealous," Sanj said.

"Of what?"

"My life has possibilities. I may have had a rocky start here in New York, but I guarantee I have a bright future. What does your future hold? Getting fat in your parents' house in West Virginia? Another failed attempt at fucking community college? Sitting on the couch with your brother, smoking pot? You'll never be anything other than a loser."

Sanj took a step back, looked her up and down—the way The Jasmines had when she first arrived, the way so many had over the past four years—and said with disgust, "Look at you."

He stormed out of the house and toward the station to catch a train into the city. The LIRR was empty, as it usually was this time of day. No one was taking the train into the city; rush hour was long over. Sanj had a whole row to himself; in fact, he practically had the whole car to himself. He lay down across the seats, on his side, curling his body into the smallest ball he could manage. He wanted to disappear. Was it true, what Sylvie had said? Did everyone know? Had everyone always known?

When he arrived at Penn Station, he pulled on his headphones, and started walking. The city still seemed so strange to him. He tried to imagine what it had been like for his father arriving in Oklahoma at age seventeen. How many times must his father have stopped in the middle of the sidewalk, seeing the houses and the lawns and the trees and the cars in the driveways, and, remembering his village, wondered, "Why am I here?"

Sanj looked around. Without realizing it, he'd wandered over to Bryant Park, where he'd often spent time when he was pretending to be at work. Over the summer, several days in a row, Sanj had noticed a South Asian homeless man, which shocked and surprised him. He was more accustomed to the Indians in their mansions in Mulberry Hills. Several times Sanj tried approaching the homeless man, often with his handheld tape recorder, but the man always retreated. Sanj wanted to ask him what it was like for him. "How do you survive?" Now the man was nowhere to be found. Summer was over. It was fall, the first in seventeen years when Sanj wasn't preparing to go back to school.

He sat down by the statue of Gertrude Stein. He'd admired her work when he'd read it in college in a twentieth-century literature class. The statue's artist had rendered Stein round and sage as a Buddha, her eyes cast downward. Sanj remembered a quote, which he now imagined Stein leaning over and whispering to him: "A real failure does not need an excuse. It is an end in itself." When he'd read the quote in class, he'd instantly felt a connection, and had scribbled it on the cover of his lit notebook; it seemed appropriate, since, though he wasn't quite failing the class, he wasn't doing particularly well, either. Still, Sanj wasn't quite sure what the quote meant.

First L.A., now New York: Sanj's attempts at carving out a life for himself had been failures. He thought of his father. He had come to a new world and built a life in the unlikeliest of places. He'd constructed a mansion, erected a fountain, encircled it with scenes from his life. Sanj couldn't even manage to keep an unpaid internship.

"A better life," his father had said. When Sanj pressed him about what that meant, Bipin said, "More opportunities for myself and for your mother. But mostly for you, my darling son." He had held out his hands, as if offering a gift. "It's all for you."

It was eight by the time Sanj returned to Long Island. The house seemed particularly quiet. He could hear clattering dishes from the dining room. He found the family there—Lala, Chandu, The Jasmines—along with Sylvie, eating dinner. Sanj sat down. Lala had already set his place, even piling the plate with food. Little was said at dinner, but Sanj couldn't help feeling that he was being stared at. The Jasmines shot him harsh glances, narrowing their eyes. Had Sylvie told them? Had they told Chandu Uncle? Lala Auntie?

After dinner, Sanj found Sylvie in Meghana's bedroom. She was sitting alone on the large, queen-size bed, curled up on top of the pink duvet, reading. She looked up from her book for a moment, but then went back to reading.

"I'm so, *so* sorry," Sanj said. He realized how insincere it must have sounded. It seemed to have become a mantra in their relationship, Sanj saying over and over to Sylvie *sorry, sorry, sorry*.

He noticed that she had packed her suitcase. "Are you leaving?"

Sylvie didn't answer. He couldn't believe the horrible things he'd said to her. He wondered if his father and Chandu Uncle had ever fought those first years in America. Surely, they must have. Had they hurt one another? How had they mended it?

"Please stay," Sanj said. As he formed the words, he realized how desperately he meant it—not for Sylvie's sake, but for his own. "Please don't leave me here alone."

He said, "Or maybe, if you're going back to West Virginia, I'll come with you."

Sylvie put down her book. "No," she said. "You can't."

Sanj stood in the doorway, blinking. He understood.

Downstairs, Lala was sitting in the living room, reading a Gujarati-language newspaper. Sanj sat down next to her. They were silent. They had nothing to say to each other, no common language to speak.

At first, Lala didn't look at him. Sanj sat quietly for a minute or two, and then found himself, almost without knowing it, scooting a little closer to her. Sanj felt his eyes well up with tears. Lala put her newspaper down, and looked at him. Her eyes were soft. She lowered her lids slightly. She opened up her right arm, and Sanj slid in, eventually resting his head on her shoulder. She held him.

He knew he would have to call his father and tell him everything. Safe in Lala's arms, he imagined it now. He would say, "Dad, I need to talk to you." His father would be in the enormous living room, which was a sunken room, two steps down from the rest of the level, making the already high ceilings even higher. He and Sanj's mother would be sitting on the sofa—a divan, really, with red brocade. They'd be watching a Bollywood movie, as they often did in the evenings, the videocassettes shipped to them from the Indian grocery store in Columbus. So many of the Bollywood films Sanj had seen had the same plot—a boy falls in love with a girl, but his parents have already fixed up an engagement to someone else, have already planned out another life for him—and this one would be no different. Bipin would pause the movie and say, "Tell us. We're listening." Sanj would be on speakerphone, and he would try his best to make his voice heard, to not let the cavernous house swallow him.